KISSING THE SUSPECT

A MYSTICAL MELVILLE NOVEL

KIMBERLY FROST

D0871657

FROSTFICTION

C allie Melville was wanted by the law, but to put it that way made things sound worse than they were. She hoped. The rumors she'd heard about the new police chief didn't make her look forward to their meeting.

Callie stood in the shadow of the Granger Falls police department with her auburn hair blowing and lamented the way her day was going. The trouble had started even before she'd woken up, but she wasn't going to think about the premonition right now. She had a bigger issue at the moment. A seventy-five-pound-dog issue.

Rufus had never cared for police stations, which Callie felt was irrational. Despite some reckless choices on Rufus's part, he wasn't the one the police had summoned. In fact, the only time the police had looked for him in the past, it had been to give him a medal usually reserved for police dogs.

Callie stood with an arm resting on top of the open car door and looked down at him. It was impossible to tell what unholy mongrel mix of breeds he was. In addition to really unattractive features, his troubled puppyhood had left him with several starbursts of scar tissue and only half of his left ear. Even as a pup he'd caused young children, who usually adored puppies, to pause and take a step back.

The vet suspected he was part bull terrier, possibly mixed with mastiff and something else. He had a huge skull and a wide, flat face, making his head a two-tone bowling ball of dirty white and muddy gray. It was safe to say that Purina commercials weren't in his future, but Rufus had other qualities.

"Seriously, Ruf, if I close this door and go in alone, you'd better not change your mind and go nuclear on this car."

Rufus liked riding in the car, provided it was moving. He didn't, however, care to be left in it when it was parked. Callie suspected it made him feel imprisoned, which Rufus had no patience for. He had been known to tear seat covers and puncture the dashboard as many as forty times in the span of fifteen minutes. He also didn't care for collars, leashes, or fences.

Rufus stared past her at the police station, making no move to escape the car.

"Ok, I'll be right back." She took the bone from the dash and set it at his feet on the seat. "Be cool."

She closed the door, popped the trunk open and took out the large shopping bag. She'd met Chief Pell once before at the retirement party for his predecessor. Physically, the new chief was a mechanical pencil of a man, tall, thin, rigidly straight and precise. His painfully thin frame was probably due to a high metabolism and was definitely none of Callie's business, but she couldn't resist bringing her wares to the meeting. She carried a large handle bag filled with her honey-glazed ham and goat cheese turnovers, honey-toasted vegetable popovers, and honey hazelnut fudge.

Inside the station, she set the largest box on the police chief's desk before handing the bag filled with four smaller ones to a grateful deputy who hustled out.

"No need to bring food, Miss Melville," Chief Pell said, setting the box to the side without a second glance. "I know that you were friendly with the former police chief, but I plan to run things my way. We won't be needing any help from supposedly psychic beekeepers."

"That's not up to you," she said calmly, channeling her cousin Lotus, who was rarely offended when someone insulted her. Lotus didn't rattle because she just didn't give a damn what anyone thought of her. Callie admired that talent, especially today.

"It certainly is up to me. I'm the chief of police," he snapped.

She blinked, thinking it was a good thing that Rufus had stayed in car. Unlike Lotus, Rufus was easily offended. Raised voices directed at Callie were high on the list of things Rufus did not tolerate.

"Listen, Chief Rudy was a great old guy in a lot of ways, but I know he was a little too free with his praise. He thought it added to the region's charm to share some wild stories about the Mystical Melville cousins, as he called us. The truth is that I've never sought recognition. None of us has. So if that's your concern, please understand that no one has to know that I'm providing information—"

"You're right. There will never be another story about Honeycakes Melville and her faithful hound helping the law find missing children. This isn't a cartoon."

"He's not a hound. As least not as far as the vet can tell. And my business is called—"

"Whatever! We don't need your so-called information. We'll collect our own information from verifiable sources. That's called investigating, and it's what we're trained to do as policemen. No need for Ouija boards or crystals."

She rolled her eyes. "Listen—"

"No, you listen," he said, raising his voice again. "Unless you witness a crime *in person* or are the victim of a crime, I don't expect to see you in this office again."

"Fine with me," she said, swiveling and striding out.

"Hang on," he said, pursuing her. "You also won't be showing up for any search parties or at any crime scenes."

She shoved the door open and walked outside. She didn't think he could legally block her from joining a volunteer search party, but she had no intention of arguing about it. She didn't take orders from the police chief or anyone else. There was only one power that she had to answer to. The one that sent the visions.

"Did you hear me, Miss Melville?" Chief Pell demanded.

Rufus jumped to attention, his paws on the passenger window glass as he growled and bared his teeth.

"Don't yell. My dog doesn't like it."

"Good God, that's an ugly dog. What kind of dog is that?" he asked, momentarily stunned, as most people were, at the sight of Rufus.

"Loyal," she said. "As the day is long. And accomplished. He's found two missing kids. That's two more than you, right? So *the best*, that's the kind of dog he is."

"And violent. You'd better keep him under control."

"He's not violent."

"Didn't he bite Larry McIntry's dog?"

"Self-defense," she said flatly.

"Bull! And doesn't he tree every cat within a twelve-block radius?"

"When provoked."

"Provoked? Exactly what do these cats do to provoke him?"

"Cat things," she said with a shrug.

"I don't care that you and your dog got lucky and discovered a couple of lost kids that I'm sure would've been found by other searchers eventually. The days of your dog running wild are over."

Rufus barked madly and butted his head against the glass like he'd come through it any second.

The chief made a show of unsnapping his holster and glaring back at Rufus.

Callie stepped in front of the passenger door to block their line of sight. "To shoot Rufus, you'd have to go through me, and gunning down an unarmed beekeeper might be hard to explain your first week on the job." Callie reached back and rapped her knuckles on the glass, saying over her shoulder, "Rufus, relax. I'm fine."

The dog growled, but the wild barking ceased.

"See you around, Chief."

He glowered, but eventually, when she did nothing but wait, he turned and walked away. Only when he was safely back in the station and out of sight did Callie walk around the car and get in the driver's seat.

Rufus sat back, but his gaze stayed fixed on the building.

"That went great, Ruf." she said, starting the car. "I think we charmed him as no other citizens have in a long time."

Callie pulled away from the curb, shaking her head. It had been the former chief's idea that she come to him immediately whenever a new recurring dream began. He'd wanted to brief his men on the details and alert them to be vigilant. Chief Rudy thought it might uncover evidence that could prevent or at least lead to rapid resolutions of impending crimes. It had almost worked. The police had mobilized and been within a mile of where she and Rufus had ultimately found the lost two-year-old child eight months ago. The little boy had wandered out in the dead of night. He was already hypothermic when she found him.

If she hadn't woken from the dream and known to start a search, it would've ended in tragedy. Tommy Walker had been the one she'd seen face down in the creek. He'd only been six feet from the water when Rufus had caught up to him. They'd barely made it in time.

Her dog had blocked the little boy's progress and then bumped him down to the ground, lying over him to keep him warm until she'd gotten there. The exhausted little guy hadn't even screamed about the smelly dog's heavy bulk on top of him.

"Rufus, you beautiful beast," she'd exclaimed, hugging her dog before dragging him off the disheveled bundle. "It's steak all week for you," she'd said, so relieved she'd been teary-eyed. They'd saved a toddler from drowning.

The new police chief was a jerk, but Callie doubted there'd be a way to avoid him. The universe had things to say, and the Melvilles knew to listen. Each of them that had a gift had learned the hard way that to ignore or abuse a mystical gift led to terrible consequences.

Most days, Callie was a beekeeper and casual organic farmer. She spent her Friday nights baking honey cakes and making fudge or roasting vegetables for a variety of flavored popovers and pot pies. Saturdays and Sundays, she ran booths at farmers' markets. Her booth was popular, and she loved seeing her regular customers and meeting new ones. Callie chatted, drank coffee, took suggestions for new recipes, and sold every bit of whatever she made. It was a great way to spend a weekend, and she never missed setting up her booth. Unless, that is, a dream became reality.

When a premonition event happened, she wasn't a beekeeper or organic food artisan. She was a Melville who'd survived a storm. When called, storm survivors had to stop everything and answer the universe's dark message.

She'd been dream-free for eight months. Then the night sent her a new vision. And this one didn't have a lost toddler who'd pushed open an unlatched door and wandered away from home. This dream featured a hulking man and a teen girl. Callie hadn't seen enough yet to know what would happen, but she knew the possibilities left her in a cold sweat. The timing of Chief Rudy's retirement was the worst. If ever Callie could've used the police's help, it was now. Instead, all she had were visions, a newly purchased stun gun, and a rough, ugly dog named Rufus.

2

No one, other than his grandmother, called Greg Brinkman Greg. He'd done three tours in the Middle East and had earned the nickname Brink because that's where he and the other Marines in his unit liked to take things. Up to the brink. And beyond.

The new kid at the desk of his gym had called him Greg *again* and was offering to show him how to use a new piece of equipment that was "wicked on the pecs." Unsolicited advice to a guy who could clearly out-lift you? Not cool. Plus, the kid had probably been a toddler around the time thirty-nine-year-old Brink got his first gym membership.

"I'm good," Brink said, holding out his hand for his membership card. He really had to get around to outfitting the home gym now that he'd finished renovating.

"Sure, Greg, but let me know if you need anything," the kid said, trying way too hard.

Brink cocked a brow and slid the membership card into his wallet as he made his way to the locker room. There was a lot of young blood in the gym these days.

Brink shoved his stuff in a locker and went to the weight

room to get down to business. For twenty years when he'd been active military personnel, staying strong and fit had been part of his job. He ran for cardio and lifted six days a week. The habit was as ingrained as brushing his teeth or showering. In the early days of civilian life the routine had helped him adjust. It made him feel like himself. After a year he could have altered things but didn't feel the need to. The time in the weight room set the tone for his day.

He lifted heavy until he could lift no more. He knew all the guys who were regulars. They spotted each other with a minimum of conversation. But a hush fell over the gym now that was deeper than usual. The couple of guys who were normally vocal as they worked out fell silent. Staring at the ceiling, he grimaced. Heather's daughter Ashleigh had arrived. Predictably, a moment later, she asked, "Brink, can you spot me?"

"I can when I'm done," he said without turning his head to look at Ashleigh. He didn't hurry, hoping the teenager might wander away. She'd asked him what gym he worked out at, and he'd made the mistake of telling her. He'd been clear that the members were almost all men, and they were pretty hardcore. He'd expected it to put her off.

Instead, she'd shown up a week later, wearing a plunging tank top and transparent peach yoga pants that looked a size too small. Workouts had initially ground to a halt as most of the guys in the place stopped to check her out. After a single glance, Brink had tried to avoid looking at her at all, but her frequent attempts to get his help or advice didn't make it easy to ignore her.

In the locker room, the conversation about her had been crude. Brink quickly shut it down, letting the guys know the girl was underage. One of the guys countered that the gym's membership age was eighteen.

"Then she lied. She's sixteen. Fact," Brink had said grimly. Ashleigh was the daughter of a woman he'd gone to high school with.

"What's the deal? 'Cause you didn't seem to have a problem spotting her. Maybe she's eighteen and you want her for yourself," Dave, a married guy pushing fifty, had said.

Brink had itched to raise his middle finger and say what the hell is it to you, married man? "She's a *kid* from my neighborhood."

"Doesn't look like a kid," Dave had countered to the surreptitious nods of some other guys.

"If Brink says she's a kid, she is," Cobie had said, putting an end to the discussion.

Brink had nodded, but he wasn't sure the other guys would allow themselves to be convinced. He knew their interest in her shouldn't have been his problem, but he felt like it was since he was the reason she'd come in the first place.

Now as he did his reps, he heard other guys approach and offer to spot for Ashleigh. He tensed, hearing the innocent way she flirted and joked with them. They lingered, but she didn't take them up on their offers. She waited for him, which was a good thing, even if it would screw up his own workout.

He finally sat up and got off the bench. But when he looked over at her, he was surprised. The see-through yoga outfits were gone. She was wearing a loose T shirt with the phrase *Messy Hair Don't Care* on it and a pair of black sweats. She also didn't have a ton of makeup on her face. Without it, she looked as young as she was.

"You look ready to sweat," he said with a smile.

She beamed and nodded. "I needed new workout

clothes. The others were old and small and not really...I got a couple things to help me fit in better here."

He wasn't sure she'd ever blend in, but he liked that she was trying to get into the place's vibe.

"Come on," he said, nodding toward the bench. "Show me what you got."

He had no idea why she was so interested in training when he did, but it seemed like it was going to be a regular thing unless he put a stop to it. He'd dropped plenty of hints that he liked to work out alone, but she'd ignored those.

She adjusted the weight on the bar and then got on the bench. It was heavier than she'd tried on other days. She widened her blue eyes as her arms shook under the bar's weight.

"You got it," Brink said, keeping his hands ready. "C'mon. Push," he said.

She strained, her face a mask of concentration, and raised the bar.

"Good," he said.

"Should I go lighter? So I can do more reps?"

"You could."

"Should I?"

He shook his head.

She took a deep breath and did four more reps. The fifth time she couldn't raise the weight.

He took it and set it back on the rack. "Good."

She got off the bench and shook out her arms, smiling. "That's my heaviest ever."

He nodded. He lifted a free weight to curl and in a moment, she followed his lead. There was a minute of welcome silence.

She nodded at his faded shirt, which had The United States Marine Corps seal resting over his heart.

"You really broke that shirt in. How old is it?"

"About your age."

She laughed. "You might want to retire it. Or does it have, like, sentimental value?"

"I'm not sentimental about clothes," he said.

"Are you sentimental about anything?" she asked.

What kind of question was that?

"Not particularly," he murmured, thinking again that he really had to get that home gym set up.

3

Callie woke in the early morning hours from another dark dream of the menacing approach of a large man shadowed in darkness, of a young girl screaming, of a body hitting the ground. More importantly, she'd seen a main street she recognized and had seen the girl near a house with a large blue truck. She'd also gotten a glimpse of some sort of military seal in the window and the first two letters of the license plate.

She bolted from her bed, damp with sweat, her heart hammering.

Rufus, who'd been asleep on the floor near his dog pillow, raised his head, scented the air and looked around.

"Morning, Ruf." Callie dug through a dresser drawer, yanking out jeans and a sweater.

Rufus rose and walked to the door.

"You don't have to come. I saw something in my dream that I want to check out. Nothing dangerous. You can go back to sleep."

Rufus made no response. He simply waited for her.

"Okay, suit yourself," she said, hurrying downstairs. She

made herself a mocha since morning had its priorities whether she was going to canvas a neighborhood for the scene of a future abduction or not.

She poured the hot liquid into a pink-and-gold ceramic to-go cup with the Honey Buzz logo on the side. She wished she was up early to spend the day in the garden, but she had to admit she was a little excited. After she'd finally accepted that the "Melville Curse" couldn't be exorcised from her body, she'd decided to view it as a gift. She'd use it to do as much good as she could. After a couple successful rescues, she'd come to feel grateful for it. Of course, those recent successes had been about finding kids who'd gotten accidentally lost. This new recurring dream was about something else entirely, something sinister and ugly.

Outside, Rufus took the front passenger seat, and she drove five miles to the wooden gazebo with West Elm outdoor furniture. This was the area she'd seen in the dream, and she was pretty sure that her vantage point was from a vehicle traveling northwest.

At six-fifteen, the sun wasn't yet up, but the horizon's glow meant it wasn't far off. She hoped to drive up and down the streets coming off the main drag before anyone was awake and out of their houses. If she spotted the truck she'd seen, maybe she'd find the girl who would get taken or the man who would take her. Either way, it was a great starting point for her investigation.

She had driven down three streets when a pair of tall headlights caused her to pull into a spot between parked cars. She idled in place, knowing the other driver would have no reason to suspect anything was unusual since there wasn't room for them to pass each other with parked cars on either side of the street.

As the truck approached, Callie froze. It was a deep

shimmering blue and had an extended cab, just like the truck from her dream. Sensing the sudden tension, Rufus leaned toward the dash and growled under his breath.

Callie followed the truck with her eyes as it passed. There was something in the back window that might have been a military decal. She craned her neck, her forehead pressed against the glass. If it turned down another street, she'd have to hurry to follow it. If it was the abductor, she didn't want him to get his truck in his garage before she saw where he lived. And it probably was him because how many young women drove monster trucks?

The truck turned a corner, heading north. Callie whipped her head to look over her shoulder as she pulled out quickly.

She jammed her foot down on the gas, and the car jerked forward. She looked sharply from side to side. She didn't want to run over some unsuspecting person who'd come out early to put out their trash. That wouldn't be a good start to anyone's day.

She swung around the corner and then nearly slammed on her brakes. She'd found where he lived! A few houses from the end of the block there was an open overhead garage door revealing the blue truck inside. A man climbed out of the cab with a duffle bag, and her breath caught.

Good God, he was huge! Was he human? Or a terminator?

She rolled past, turning her head just as he looked her way. Seriously, cyborg was not out of the realm of possibilities. She went around the corner and parked, her heart racing.

"Did you see him, Rufus? What's up with that? Is it steroids, do you think?" The man's muscles had totally outgrown his body. He would've needed to be eight feet tall to carry that much bulk around. She shook her head. "You know, I bet he was coming home from the gym. The sun's not even up," she said in amazement. "That's beyond dedication. It's gotta be an obsession. Because why does anyone need to get that big and ripped? To carry off a teen girl while she's still in her car? To be cast as a live-action version of The Hulk? It's crazy."

She paused, wondering what her next step should be. She'd never investigated a would-be kidnapper before. Or anyone else for that matter.

"I need to start simple. If he takes the girl, there are two possibilities of how he'll proceed. He'll either keep her prisoner somewhere or he'll abuse her and kill her." Callie shuddered, feeling her stomach churn. It was one thing to swoop in to help find a woman or child after the person had gone missing. It was something else entirely to imagine the horrible things that might happen to the victim of an abduction if Callie didn't stop it. She wasn't mentally prepared to deal with that kind of pressure. But she didn't have a choice. She had to try to protect the girl she'd seen in the vision.

Rufus barked and then leaned forward and licked her face.

"Thanks, dog," she whispered, rubbing the saliva off her cheek. "Just don't go soft on me, Ruf. This guy is really big and really mean. We are going to have to be tough and smart if we want to save the girl. Especially if we want to get her away from him before he has a chance to do anything to her, which we do. We need to be fast. Faster than we've ever been, and I'm not sure how much time we have to prepare because the dreams are coming closer together, and you know—"

Someone knocked on the roof of the car. She jumped and Rufus went wild with barking. Callie's head swiveled, but instead of spotting a malicious mountain of muscle, a woman who would never see seventy again ambled to the side of car. She lifted her cane and rapped the driver's window with its handle.

"What the hell?" Callie mumbled.

Rufus, undeterred by the interloper's advanced age, snarled between barking.

Callie put a hand out to push Rufus back into his seat and lowered her window a couple of inches. She did not want to leave enough room for Rufus's big jaws to snap through.

"Hello," Callie said, though she doubted the woman could hear her over Rufus's stream of what were surely canine curses.

"Girl, you need to muzzle that dog," the woman snapped.

Callie was immediately annoyed on Rufus's behalf. The woman had smacked the car with her cane and startled them. It was normal for a startled dog to react by barking.

"Rufus doesn't care for muzzles."

"What does that have to do with it? He'll wake the neighborhood."

Rufus, who'd sized the woman up, must have decided he could take her without intimidating her first, so he quieted.

"That's better. My goodness that's a horrible dog. What's he doing riding in the front seat? What's he doing in your car period? You should keep him chained in your own yard. Or have your neighbors complained too much? Is that why you've transported him here? Well, we won't stand for it."

Wow, Callie thought. This morning was a lot to handle on only one cup of coffee.

"He wasn't barking at all until you assaulted my car.

You had better not have dented my roof," Callie said. She'd found that going on the offensive was often a good defense.

"I didn't dent anything. Now, about why I've come out here. I thought it was you, Miss HoneyBuns."

"My business is called Honey Buzz."

"That's a silly name."

"People like it."

"Says who?"

"People."

"I'm people. I don't like it."

"The first rule of business is that you can't please everyone. Goodbye now," Callie said, rolling up the window.

The cane rapped on the glass. Rufus barked a protest.

"What the hell?" Callie muttered, lowering the window a few inches.

The woman leaned forward. "I want yellow cabbage roses. Two plants in two-gallon buckets."

What? It surprised Callie, but the woman obviously knew who she was and that she'd once supplied local nurseries with bushes and vines she'd grown. Callie had been in the paper several times over the past few years, so she guessed it shouldn't be totally unexpected that she'd be recognized locally. "I don't sell roses anymore, ma'am."

"I know. Stop fooling around baking cakes and get back to those plants. There are plenty of baked goods in the world. Too many. What we need is more giant yellow roses. Starting with my yard."

"I—" Callie took a breath and exhaled. "I'm flattered that you liked my rose plants, but I really don't have time to—"

"I don't want excuses; I want roses. The yellow ones with the peach tips."

"The sunset blend. Those are very pretty. You can visit

the town's botanical gardens in fall and buy blooms or cuttings."

"I don't want cuttings. I want plants. Two of them in two-gallon planters. I know what I want and that's it. Don't make me write to the governor. My hands are old and gnarled. I don't care to write personal notes anymore, except under extreme circumstances. Like sending condolences to families who have lost a boy over there fighting hoodlum terrorists."

Callie stared at the woman. The conversation was taking a bizarre turn. Was the woman senile? If so, was she supposed to be out on her own? Callie glanced around, looking for an open front door or gate. "Hoodlum terrorists? That's really two different things I think."

"They rig bombs to go off in the streets and everywhere else. That's hoodlum behavior if I ever heard of it. I'd like to get my hands on the one who almost killed my grandson. I'd take more than an earlobe by God."

Rufus leaned forward and barked, possibly approvingly.

"Rufus, don't encourage her. Ma'am, where do you live? Is there someone—?"

"Never mind about that. You're just a honeybuns girl who can't even figure out that she's supposed to be a gardener. What would you know about fighting the enemy?"

"Not much," Callie said, deciding that being agreeable would end the conversation sooner. The woman couldn't be seriously demented if she knew who Callie was, could she? No, Callie doubted it. The old woman was just eccentric apparently.

"When can you deliver my plants?"

"I don't know. I'll have to see."

The woman huffed. "Never mind then. I'll just send my grandson to pick them up."

The old lady was relentless!

Callie sighed. "Ma'am, there's nothing to pick up. I'm not selling plants at the moment."

"Well, how many bushes do you have?"

"None. I'm not selling—"

"Not for sale! You personally. You have all those acres. How many cabbage rose bushes?"

"What does that have to do with it?"

"I'll buy two of your bushes. My grandson will dig them up and replant them in my yard. All you need to do is take a check since you're too busy making cakes to do what you should be doing. Oregon doesn't need any more test gardens. All those hybrid growers using our sun and soil to grow their roses that they'll sell in other states. We need roses right here! I believe I will write the governor. Maybe he can talk some sense into you."

"Ma'am—"

"I'll send the boy to get them. What will it cost? Two hundred dollars a bush? Highway robbery, but what choice do I have? I'll be dead soon, and I can't wait forever while you're figuring out that you're not meant to be a cake baker."

Callie burst out laughing. Rufus cocked his head and narrowed his black eyes.

"You don't have to send anyone. If you want those rose plants so badly, I'll see that you get some."

"And return to gardening full-time?"

"No."

The old woman sniffed. "Well, the bushes will have to do. For now. Here comes Greg and what does he have in his hand? A bag from a bakery. See how easy it is to get baked goods in this town? Brownies, donuts, danishes...anything you want, any day of the week. But what you don't see him carrying is a rose as big as his fist. Because those you can't get anywhere. There's only one person in the area that can breed those roses."

"Well soon, you can too—oh my God."

The grandson wasn't a boy. He was the monster man of the monster truck.

Having sensed Callie's shock, Rufus growled.

"Morning," the man said to his granny before turning his attention to the car. He looked past Callie at Rufus.

Rufus glared at him.

The man leaned down. He smelled like aftershave, which was another surprise. Callie hadn't really thought about what he would smell like, but if pressed she would've guessed stale sweat and malignant rage against women. Instead he smelled wonderful.

"What's wrong?" he asked Rufus in a low voice that reverberated like a bass drum.

Rufus leaned forward and cocked his head, teeth still bared.

The man mimicked the head tilt, exposing the tips of his own teeth and causing Callie to press back against her seat. She noticed that the man's right earlobe was gone. There was also a small puncture scar on his cheek and a thin slice of a scar on his neck. His head was shaved so there was just a shadow of stubble. He was Rufus in human form, except better looking. But no, she told herself, correcting her thoughts. The man wasn't like her dog because Rufus helped save people. He didn't abduct and hurt them.

Rufus stopped snarling but watched the man for any sudden moves.

The man hooked his fingertips on the edge of the partially open driver's side window. Half of the guy's left pinkie was gone. Where had he lost it? Fighting hoodlum terrorists? Callie clenched her teeth, trying not to wonder whether there were some things to admire about this man. No, no matter what he'd done and been through in the military, it did not give him the right to do whatever he wanted with a young woman.

Rufus leaned forward and licked the man's hand.

"Good dog," the man said.

"That dog is a menace," the pushy granny said. "She can't control him. He's not the sort of a dog for a pretty girl-gardener. You should take that dog, Greg. You could keep him in line. She needs a Labrador or a golden retriever. Anyone with sense can see that. Or maybe a smaller dog altogether. But not the kind with a snippy bark, for heaven's sake. They're irritating."

The man grinned.

"I'm going in," the woman announced. "Bring the honey gardener for breakfast, but not the dog. He stays in the yard. He can have the leftover bacon if he doesn't bark down the fences. The neighbors wouldn't like that, and who could blame them?"

The octogenarian turned and started off with unexpected swiftness for someone with osteoporosis and a cane.

Callie blinked.

"Greg Brinkman. It's Brink to my friends."

"What is it to your enemies?" she asked lightly.

"I wouldn't know."

"Because they don't live to tell you?" she murmured.

"Not if I did my job right."

"How long did you serve?"

"Twenty years."

Callie's mind raced. That was longer than she'd expected. Had he enlisted at eighteen? And then what? In combat units, he wouldn't have had the time and privacy to develop a routine that involved abduction. Was this going to be a new hobby for him? Or was there something special about the girl in question? Did he know her? Was she from the neighborhood? The daughter of a friend, maybe?

"Thank you for your service," Callie said, hoping her face didn't give away the true direction of her thoughts.

"My pleasure. So are you coming to breakfast?"

She swallowed. She did not want to have breakfast with this man and his crazy, cranky grandmother. But she did need to investigate him, and what better opportunity would she get to interrogate him?

"It was lovely of her to invite me. Yes, I'll come."

4

His grandmother had lost the girl to him, which surprised Brink. The old woman usually managed to get her own way, and if she'd invited the beautiful beekeeper to breakfast it was because she wanted to visit with her.

He'd never met anyone who listed their occupation as beekeeper. He'd figured bees mostly kept themselves, but apparently not always. He wanted to know more about her, but she was the one doing the questioning. Or at least most of it.

The young woman stood beside him in the kitchen, making biscuits and plying him with a random and sometimes bizarre assortment of queries. It gave him pause because it was vaguely reminiscent of military intelligence-gathering during the Gulf wars.

The woman wanted to know about family properties, whether he liked to hunt and fish and, if so, where? Did he have his own gear and, if so, where did he store it?

Where did he store it? She had actually asked that. Women

had asked him a lot of questions over the years, sometimes about his possessions. He'd always guessed that was them trying to learn how he lived and how much money he had. But none that he could remember had ever asked him the specifics of where he kept his fishing rods and tackle. It was odd. This woman intrigued him, with her smattering of light brown freckles and luminous blue eyes that followed his every move like he might make the bacon stand up and do tricks.

Through the kitchen window he watched her dog run the length of his grandmother's yard, test the fence for gaps, and then bound onto the top of the picnic table to gain a vantage point from which to check out the other yards. Brink bet he was assessing his ability to clear the fence and which direction he'd go when he did.

"I take it your dog is a rescue. Did he get those scars from abuse or from fighting?"

"I don't know. Abuse I think."

"Where'd you get him? The humane society?"

"No, from a ditch near I-84."

He whistled. "How many people has he bitten?"

"One."

"Good reason?"

"He obviously thought so."

"Did you?"

"It would've probably been better if he'd threatened to call the police on the guy, but Rufus doesn't have a cell phone."

"What was the guy doing?"

"Beating up his son."

"Got it." He paused. "I thought the dog might have been protecting you."

She glanced out the window to study Rufus. "I feel sorry

for any guy who tries to hurt me while that dog's around. And vice versa."

He smiled. "So I guess you're not giving him to me after all."

This made her smile, and he was more glad to see it than he'd have expected.

"Rufus likes you, which is surprising. When you put your hand through the window, I thought you might lose more fingertips. You're quite a risk taker."

He glanced at the shortened pinkie with its scarred blunt end. "A fingertip? Wouldn't even miss it."

She looked up at him. "You've been through a lot. Pain doesn't scare you much, huh? Normal consequences that would stop other people from doing things probably wouldn't deter you?"

He liked the way she watched him. He couldn't remember any woman ever watching him as intently as she did.

"Do you need help with something risky?" he asked.

"Like what?"

"I don't know." He took the bacon off the heat and set it aside. "You've been sizing me up. I figure you're going to ask me to do something. Maybe an old boyfriend won't give you back your stuff? Or a coworker's giving you a hard time?"

"Could you help that way? By intimidating someone?" Her tone was feather light, but there was sincere curiosity.

He frowned. So she *was* hoping to use him, even though she didn't know a thing about him and whether he might take intimidating someone too far. She was also hoping to use him when they weren't even friends. He'd seen the type before. They wanted drama; some women liked to see men fight over them. It was all about stroking their own egos and seeing what they could get a man to give them or to do for them. He didn't want her to be one of those women. He'd wanted her to be interested in him for himself, not as some meathead who was good with his fists.

He turned and grabbed three plates. "No, I wouldn't intimidate someone as a favor to you. Or to anyone."

"So why do you work out so much? What's the point of getting that strong unless it's to scare people? Or to fight with them?"

"Some guys bulk up to compete as professional body-builders."

"Is that why you do it?"

"No," he admitted.

"Then why?"

"It's a habit."

He glanced over his shoulder and found her gaze trained on him, intense and interested. There was something off about this woman. He needed to take a step away. Unfortunately, he couldn't make himself do it. He had the same reaction to her that he'd had going into battle. It was a fire in the belly that made him welcome more flames.

"But it doesn't have to be a habit. You choose to make it one. Why?"

"When I was a Marine, I needed to know I could drag a fallen brother in full gear out of a kill zone. I needed to know that in hand-to-hand combat the enemy wouldn't kill me without dying himself. None of them was going to get by me alive to kill another guy in my unit. Now there's no enemy, but I guess after so many years of needing to be in that kind of shape, it's just what I do. I have to push myself hard. It's who I am."

"Your body's a weapon," she said thoughtfully.

He shrugged. "I doubt I'll ever use it that way again in civilian life, but it doesn't hurt to be ready. What if there was an active shooter situation or some other emergency? I might need to step up. I sure as hell wouldn't want to fall short because I'd slacked off at the gym or the range."

"Once a Marine, always a Marine," she murmured.

He nodded.

"Are you ever worried you'll go too far?"

"At the gym?"

"No. Like in a situation where your temper got the best of you?"

"My temper doesn't get the best of me."

"Good to know," she said, never taking her eyes off his face.

Sometimes in battle his awareness of the enemy had been laser focused, and everything that was of no consequence ceased to exist. That solitary connection that forced everything else out of mind had never happened in civilian life before. It was happening now. He waited silently for her to ask him something else. Or for her to tell him something about herself, or about what she wanted him to do for her. God knows he wanted to do things for her. And to her.

Instead the spell was broken by his grandmother's voice from the other room. "What's happened to the bacon? Pig's escaped, and there's a shortage?"

Callie laughed. "She is really something."

"This is nothing. When the Seahawks lost the Super Bowl, she swung her cane like a bat and took out the stereo and two rows of antique china."

"My God."

"Exactly. The decent hold I've got on my temper? Not inherited."

She laughed again, and he could relate to the dog in the yard. Rufus could've cleared the fence easily and been in the next county before anyone caught up to him, but the dog ignored the instinct to run free. It would've meant leaving this girl behind, and what guy would want to do that?

Brink stiffened, wondering at the strange course of his thoughts. He wasn't the type to jump into things with a woman he'd just met. He reminded himself that he had plans that were in motion, and he was on a tight timeline. The reminder didn't dampen his reaction to her though when she leaned forward, and he caught her pumpkin spice scent. His muscles and more reacted, impairing his decision-making. In an instant, he'd made up his mind to explore where things would go with the strange blue-eyed beekeeper.

5

Callie went home and took a two-hour nap in which she dreamed about Brink. It wasn't a premonition; in the visions there was a crackling sound, like static, that constantly hummed. She rarely heard anything above it. Normal dreams were filled with conversations and the sounds of normal life, so this was odd.

She woke, feeling restless and confused. She called her cousin Natalie and then worked in the garden for a few hours while awaiting Nat's arrival. She pulled weeds that tried to encroach on her vegetables and adjusted the ties around her climbing vines. She was training some of her roses to climb her new trellises. Roses made her think of Brink's grandmother, so she turned the other direction. The bougainvilleas were in bloom, and flowers as light and delicate as tissue paper spilled over the garden arches in pastel peach and bright fuchsia. It was a lovely time of year to have a garden.

She took some cuttings from the yellow cabbage rose bushes that Mrs. Brinkman wanted. She put the cuttings in water and set them in the windowsills. They were gorgeous. She'd done a good job with them.

The doorbell rang, and Rufus shot out from the trees and raced to the house. She smiled. The dog barked its warning, and she opened the back door. Ruf darted past her and stood at the front door, noisily ready.

"Rufus, chill," she said.

Callie opened the door slowly to prevent Rufus from banging the screen door open and knocking Natalie down.

Natalie, wise to the dog's ways, tossed in a dog biscuit.

The dog studied her a moment.

"It's Natalie, Rufus. You know her," Callie said impatiently.

"Hello, Rufus," Natalie said with forced cheer.

Rufus snapped up the treat and walked off.

"Really nice, dog. She's family, you know!" Callie called.

"With that charm and those looks, I can't see why the Westminster dog show hasn't shown interest yet."

Callie laughed. "The only job offer I ever expect him to get is for a hell hound. Or maybe the lead in a Cujo remake."

Natalie grinned. "Stephen King. Have you watched Gramps's *entire* movie collection?"

"Oh, no. I'm saving the Westerns for my next bad breakup. I figure I'll be in the mood for six-shooters and revenge." Callie hugged Natalie, relishing the spicy perfume of amber, citrus, and sandalwood she wore. Natalie must have been spending the day away from the inn since she was wearing jeans and had her golden brown hair pulled up into a large crystal-encrusted hair clip. Nat's style was funky boho chic, but her mind was East Coast MBA.

"Coffee or tea?"

"I want coffee, but I should have tea," she said, chewing on her lip. Natalie had a ton of energy and too much coffee made her jittery and snappy. "Do you have any ginger-apricot?"

"Yes," Callie said, waving her into the kitchen. She warmed honey and some honey cakes, setting out butter and milk in their great grandmother's china. She set a tiered stand of cakes and treats in the center. Soon they sat across from each other at the kitchen table like they were having a tea party.

Natalie drizzled honey into her tea and said, "So let's talk. If Lotus were here, she'd say you were reckless and foolish for going alone into a strange house with a giant guy you dreamt is a killer."

"I never dreamt he was a killer."

"I stand corrected. A kidnapper. So much safer!" Nat sipped from her cup, looking over it at Callie with knowing, almond-shaped brown eyes.

"I'm not sure he's a kidnapper. Or future kidnapper. I saw his truck in one of the dreams, but I never saw the girl inside it. I never saw him grab her."

"But he's involved. And correct me if I'm wrong, but have the visions ever shown you superfluous details before?"

"No," she admitted. "In retrospect, everything I've ever seen has been important in some way."

"So, this guy is involved."

"He seems—I don't know. Not mean. Here's a man who makes his grandmother breakfast in the morning and stays in shape in case he needs to do something heroic."

"So he says. People can compartmentalize. Ted Bundy was super charming, right up until he got a girl alone."

Callie grimaced, but nodded. She pushed her slice of cake away, having lost her appetite. "I know he could be more than he seems. He probably is." Callie held her cup in both hands, trying to warm her fingers as a chill passed through her.

"I'm sorry, Cal."

"No, it's ok. I need to hear it. That's why I asked you over: for an objective opinion from someone I trust."

"I'm sorry you had breakfast with him and liked him."

"I was attracted to him I think, more than anything. I can't explain it. Maybe it was just the adrenaline and the proximity."

"Maybe it was pheromones. I blame those suckers for everything."

Callie made herself smile. "For sure."

Natalie reached across and clasped Callie's hand. "You ok?"

"Yeah, sure, of course. And actually, this is the closest I've ever gotten to identifying someone that I need to help before I actually need to help them. I don't know that fraternizing with a suspect is something I'll ever do again. I don't want to have mixed feelings about what I need to do, but I think it was important this time. And I learned something."

"You got some useful information? That's good." Natalie bit the nail of her right middle finger which was already incredibly short. The conversation was putting Nat on edge, though she was trying to appear calm.

"I know his name and where he lives. From what he said, I don't think his place has a basement or storage space for him to keep someone long-term. He lives alone, so he could have a room or something, but the neighbors are nearby. It would have to be well soundproofed. Also, his grandmother is right there and could drop by. If I had to guess, I think he'll take the girl somewhere else. He isn't a hunter—of animals, at least—so I don't know if he'd have a favorite area in the woods to take her to. But he's military. I'm sure he's used to scoping out foreign terrain and reading maps. He's strong enough to carry her wherever he'd take her and to bury her afterward." Callie put a hand to her mouth, her stomach protesting the thoughts and images that came to mind.

Callie took a couple of deep breaths and dabbed at her forehead with a napkin. She couldn't believe what a strong reaction she was having. She felt sick at the thought of Brink abducting the mystery girl.

Nat hopped up from her seat and came around the table. She put an arm around Callie's shoulders in a makeshift hug. "Hey, you don't have to do this! At least not this way."

"You know I do. There's a girl who's not safe and who won't be safe unless I figure this out in time."

"Right," Natalie said, taking a deep breath and blowing it out. "Right. I don't know what this is like. My curse hasn't been active like yours. Or Lotus's. I hope it's not as dangerous as Lo's."

"You know what Lotus's curse is?"

"No, not exactly, but I know it's dangerous from the way she keeps her distance. People she cares about have died— accidentally, but still."

"You think those deaths are related?" Callie asked.

"I don't know. I think so." Natalie shook her head, pursing her lips. "It's so unfair. To have these visions start and never let up. It's like a chronic illness. Maybe worse since there's no medication to take!"

"Yeah, it's tough sometimes. The one time when I had a dream that seemed too vague, and I didn't try to piece things together, it wasn't good. I even said something like, 'This really isn't my problem. I'll do what I can, but I'm not going to be something I'm not. I'm not a police officer, and I don't plan to act like one.' Within hours, my appendix got infected, and my mom had to be hospitalized for pneu-monia and almost died. I told Gramps what I'd said, and he pressured me to take it back. You know what he believes. The curse demands action.

"I listened to him," Callie continued. "I promised out loud to take whatever steps were necessary to follow through on the mission delivered through the dream. I made it through the surgery. My mom recovered completely in record time. Maybe it was all a coincidence, but I don't think so. My blood pressure was low before surgery. I'm not sure I would've made it off the operating room table if I hadn't changed my mind."

"Wow. You never said." Nat chewed on her fingernail.

"No. What would've been the point of scaring you? You hadn't become a storm survivor yet. You didn't need to know. Besides, I was so happy and relieved when I rescued those lost children. And I've been able to bring families closure in other cases," she murmured in a low voice. "It's a curse, but it's a gift too. I really believe that."

Natalie was silent, clearly not agreeing with the gift part. "What will you do next? And what can I do to help?"

"I'm not sure if you're allowed to play an active role, and I don't want you to be in danger if you don't need to be. But I appreciate your coming over for moral support."

"That's easy. I want to do more, Cal. There must be something," she said, sitting in the chair closest to Callie's. Natalie kept a hand on Callie's arm and squeezed for emphasis. She was such a great friend.

"Maybe," Callie said. "I always go with my instincts. So far the only time I've felt I should take someone along, it's been Rufus."

Natalie smiled. "Well I suppose if you're going into danger, what better companion than a hell hound?"

"Exactly," Callie said, smiling back.

~

ABOUT A HALF HOUR after Natalie left, Callie sat on the back porch, enjoying the smell of blooming jasmine when Rufus bounded out of the woods, dripping muddy water. He'd obviously been fishing in the pond, but she didn't see a fish, so she wondered what had brought him back to the house. Usually once he went into the water, he refused to come out without a fish unless she offered him something really tasty as an inducement.

"Again with the fishing, Ruf? You know, you're not coming in the house smelling like a swamp. You either take a bath in the metal tub, or you're sleeping on the deck. Non-negotiable."

The dog ignored her and bolted to the side of the house and down the path along the fence. His barking faded as he got farther away.

"What are you doing, dog?" she murmured, setting aside her recipe journal. She rounded the house and followed the path under the wisteria trellises to the gate.

Rufus bore no resemblance to a hound of hell as he pressed his face against the rungs of the gate and licked a figure on the other side. She paused when she was close enough to suspect who it was.

"Hello?" she called.

Greg Brinkman, Brink, glanced up and nodded. "Hey."

She joined Rufus at the gate. "If you came to steal my dog, you might want to try being more stealthy. He led me right to you."

Brink lowered his mirrored sunglasses so he could look at her with those Arctic blue eyes. "Thanks for the feedback," he said with a smirk that clearly said he didn't need advice on how to infiltrate a property.

The dog went on licking the hand that was extended through the bars.

"Rufus, what's your deal? You want a new home?" she asked.

Brink's smile widened. "It's not me he likes so much. He smells what I brought him."

"What you brought him?"

"Some leftover stew, heavy on the steak."

"Mr. Brinkman, are you courting my dog?"

He tossed his head back and laughed. "No man alive could get that dog away from you."

"Yesterday, I didn't think so. Now I'm not so sure," she mused. "So what are you doing here? Besides having a bromance with Rufus?"

"I came for the bushes."

"The bushes?" she echoed.

"The ones you sold my grandmother."

"Oh my God. She is as bold as brass, isn't she?"

"That she is," he agreed. "What are you telling me? You didn't agree to sell her some rose plants?"

"I don't actually have any of the plants for sale that she wants, which she very well knows."

He nodded. "Ok. I'll remind her." He held a heaping plastic freezer bag through the bars.

Rufus barked and jumped up. He pierced the bag with his teeth and tore it open when he dropped to the ground. The stew rained down on the cobbles.

"Wow, really, Ruf?" she asked, but the dog ignored her. He feasted on the fallen food, lapping up the meat and gravy from the stones.

"I guess that'll save on dishwashing," Brink said.

"And on the need to share," she said, giving Rufus's flank a poke.

"Do you have a trash can out here?" he asked, holding up the now empty bag.

"Sure, I'll take it."

He handed it over. "It was good to see you," he said and turned to go.

"Hang on," she said. "I suppose I can spare a rose bush or two, considering how incredibly charming your grandmother is."

He laughed.

"Fair warning though, they've been in the ground quite awhile and have put down their roots. Getting them out without damaging them will take some work."

"I don't want to tear up your landscaping. If you tell me what she wants, I'll go online and buy them for her."

"She has her heart set on mine, and she strikes me as the type of person who will never let someone forget it if she doesn't get what she thinks she was promised. Besides, I'm a little flattered by how much she likes them. I'm sure she'll give them a good home."

"She sits in her garden every day except during thunderstorms."

Callie smiled. "So they'll have company. Flowers like that," she said with a wink. "Hang on. The gate's locked. Give me a minute to get the key."

6

B rink rinsed his hands with the hose and rubbed the
excess water on his jeans. Callie wore a white
sundress, which seemed optimistic given the size
and state of her dog. On the off chance Rufus didn't wreck
the dress, which made her look like an angel, Brink himself
had no intention of leaving handprints, assuming he got the
opportunity.

Callie returned with a key on a chain and after opening
the gate, she slipped the chain over her head, the key falling
down the front of her dress into gorgeous lightly tanned
cleavage.

"So I don't lose it," she said with a wink.

"Sure," he said, thinking that he had never wanted to
take someone's keys more.

He followed her down the path to the back of her place,
watching her hips and round heart-shaped butt. Not having
taken his eyes off her, he had to force his gaze away when
she finally said, "Well, what do you think?"

He looked around and whistled. Nothing in a yard was

ever going to interest him as much as a beautiful female body, but her yard was impressive. He'd visited a botanical garden with his ex once, and Callie's garden put that place to shame.

There were explosions of spring flowers, budding bushes, and vines climbing up trellises and lining pathways. There were iron benches and sculptures, fountains, fruit trees and a pond. Intermixed there were hanging hives abuzz with activity. Through the glass sliding door, a tiered platter held an array of small cakes, jam and honey jars, and cut flowers. It was like something from a magazine.

"Impressive."

"I started with three small flowering bushes and one hive."

"How many hives now?"

"Fifteen. Not all here. I rotate them to several sites, to boost pollination in the public gardens and for a few of the local farmers."

"You're obviously successful."

She offered him the slightly crooked smile that could become the best part of a guy's day.

"I try," she said.

"And talented."

She looked up at him through her lashes, and he felt that look to the pit of his stomach and lower.

"Thank you. It's almost exactly how I want it," she said.

"Almost?"

"I like to have dinner parties at dusk and later."

He looked around and noted the lanterns with heavily burned candles. "You need professional lighting?"

"Exactly, but no one in town can do what I'm dreaming about. The estimates from out-of-town experts are expensive. Most of my profits I've poured back into the business, to grow it. So the lighting project has to wait. I'm setting aside some funds bit by bit. In a few years, I'll splurge."

"A sound strategy." *Fortune favors the bold*, he thought. He knew how to rig outdoor lighting.

She shrugged. "I hope so," she said thoughtfully. She waved for him to follow her.

They walked to a corner of the property, and she pointed to a section of large bushes.

"I have five of the blush-tipped yellow ones she likes. She can have any two." She extended a hand, pointing them out. "I know you'll be able to dig them up on your own, but you might need help to transport them in the huge terra cotta pots I've got that could hold them. The root span is pretty wide, and the roots need to be protected.

"Best if you supervise then," he said.

"Sure, do you want to come back later? Or tomorrow?"

"I will if you're busy. Or I could get to work."

"You mean now?"

He nodded.

"All right, I'm not too busy."

SHE'D THOUGHT he had too many muscles. Then he took his shirt off, and she changed her mind.

He was spectacular. He was beyond even normal action movie star buff. Instead of a terminator, he was more of a... mountain range.

He was perfectly symmetrical across his shoulders and back except on the lower left side where there was a patch of scars. One was small and circular, as if from a gunshot wound, but lower there was more extensive scarring. She wondered what had made those.

Rufus hovered nearby while Brink dug, occasionally sidling in to help. Brink rubbed the dog's head and then told him, "Go play. I've got this."

Get a grip, she told herself when she had the urge to take a bite out of him. *He could be a very bad guy. Probably is. Except why does Rufus like him? Aren't dogs supposed to be great judges of character? Also, knowing what I know, shouldn't I see some sliver of his inner nature if he's bad?*

She went back and forth in her head until it ached. Brink, oblivious, worked like a machine. When the plants were liberated to her specifications, he brought one huge pot at a time on a rolling cart. He tipped the pot onto its side, slid the plant in and in a Herculean show of strength raised it up. She added soil and water and then he rolled it into the back of his truck and secured it.

The process took a few hours. She imagined most guys couldn't have managed it all, let alone by late afternoon. When he had his shirt back on and was ready to go, she stood a couple feet from the truck.

"It's really nice of you to do this for your grandmother. You must care a lot about her."

"I do."

"Are your parents nearby, too?"

"No."

She waited a moment, but he didn't say more. "Ok, well, I hope she enjoys them."

"She will. Thanks."

She nodded.

"Take care," he said, climbing into the truck's cab.

She watched him drive away, sorry to see him go. For the

hours while he'd been in the yard, they had been on relatively neutral ground. The next time she saw him everything might be different. She'd likely have to get with the program and treat him like the enemy. She dreaded that. Completely.

7

Callie woke flushed and panting. Now *that* had been a completely different kind of premonition than she'd ever had. She wasn't even sure her spine could bend like that.

She licked her lips and stared at the ceiling. She couldn't remember much of the dream, but for once there was no doubt about the person's identity. The big bad Marine had certainly been the star of this particular dream. And she'd been there, which was also new. Had they been in a closet to start? It hadn't looked like any of her closets, and she couldn't imagine him having a stuffed souvenir whale from Sea World. So where...?

Who cares about the closet! A sexy premonition dream? Totally unprecedented.

If sexy interludes with Brink were in her future, he must not have been the hulking shadow from the earlier premonitions, right? Unless it was a warning. That would be just like a curse. Show her all the fun that she shouldn't have.

Her alarm started its incessant beeping, and she jerked to attention. She glanced at the clock. Damn. She really wanted to lie in bed to relive—er, analyze—that dream in detail. Unfortunately, there wasn't time. She dragged herself up and meandered to the shower.

Normally, she had her morning routine down to a precision operation, but this morning she was distracted and it took an extra fifteen minutes for her to get ready and load her van.

Come on. The dream wasn't that big of a deal!

She tried to force her mind to concentrate on the upcoming day. The weekend farmers' markets were the highlight of the week. She was unveiling a couple new recipes, and she always looked forward to seeing her customers. Fortunately once the farmers' market was in full swing, there would be no time to think about anything else.

Three weekends per month she stayed local and once a month she went to Portland. Arriving extra early at the local market was part of her routine so she could stop by the Hot Brew booth which featured coffee blends with beans from all over the world. Their Java Junkie morning blend was exactly what she needed. It was a mix of beans from Colombia, Papua New Guinea, and Hawaii. She poured herself a tall cup, tipping in some fresh honey that she'd put into a glass jar with a matching stir. The Honey Buzz name and logo were etched on the side. She left the honey for the Hot Brew customers and would pick up the empty jar at the end of the day. The support among Granger Falls vendors was part of what made the local farmers' market feel like a family affair.

Before she reached her booth, her friend Jan had offered her a fresh-baked ham and goat cheese croissant, which Callie happily took, promising to hold back a full-sized honey cake for her to take home to her sons, who loved them.

Callie put up her banner and set up her displays. Louis Armstrong's What a Wonderful World began to play, signaling the opening of the park's front gates. She glanced at the stacks of pink-and-gold boxes and her tiered cake stand with its bite-sized samples. She finished off the display by placing a couple of roses at the base. Perfect, she thought with a smile.

The early morning crowd that arrived at eight got first choice of everything and were often long gone by the ten-in-the-morning rush that lasted until early afternoon.

Callie took a sip of her coffee and set it behind her on a chair, greeting the morning crowd, filling orders and sharing gossip. The crowds thickened by late morning, and her leisurely pace had given way to necessarily brisk and cheerful waves to people as she filled orders quickly to keep the line moving.

Callie was surprised to see her cousin Lotus weave through the crowds. Lotus was a silent partner in both Callie and Natalie's businesses, but she did not like crowds, or as far as Callie could tell, most people.

Lotus's inky dark hair was cut to just above her shoulders in sharp spikes and a fringe of bangs swept across her forehead. Lotus might have looked goth if she'd ever worn dark lipstick or nail polish, but she never bothered. She was beautiful and exotic without makeup and had been born with criminally long eyelashes and very blue eyes. Men chased her, but only the most determined ended up with her for long. She was deceptively petite; beneath Lotus's thin frame was a strength and will usually reserved from men like, well, Brink. Callie had only seen Lotus in action once, though the stories were legendary. When she'd been younger, Callie had been sure they'd been exaggerated. But on a spring break, Lotus had gone behind a hotel to investigate the sounds of a fight. It had been a hate crime in progress, and Lotus had very coolly said to the aggressors, "If you're smart, you'll walk away." Everything that had happened next was a blur. A foot to a knee, a crunching sound, and a man going down and howling. Her sliding and snapping a pair of fingers on the other man's hand. It allowed the young man who was being beaten to get away. Lotus had backed away, too, and melted into shadows with the sounds of fury and pain fading in the background. Callie had asked Lotus several times where she'd learned to fight like that, but Lotus has been vague.

"Good morning," Callie said brightly.

"I need to rob the till. Can you spare a couple of hundred?" Lotus asked, her shimmering black hair falling to the side as she cocked her head.

"Of course," Callie said, opening the tin. "Everything okay?"

Lotus had won the lottery twice but lived like a minimalist hermit. Callie had never known her to be without money.

Lotus glanced at the sky. "Not a storm cloud in sight."

"No, I meant your needing money. Since when?"

"Oh," Lotus said with a smirk. "I'm in the middle of an all-night poker game that may go all day, too. I need a little Irish coffee and cigarette money if I'm gonna see it through. No need to worry about me. How about you? How are you, Cal? I heard you've got the dreams again."

"I'm ok. I—I had a strange one. I'll tell you about it if you're staying in town and have some time this week."

"I always have time for you," Lotus said. "Want to tell me about it now?"

Callie glanced at the line of customers snaking down the aisle.

"No, you've got your game to get back to, and I've got customers. How about tomorrow?"

"Sure." Lotus shoved some cash in the pocket of her jeans, waved, and walked away.

"Lotus, don't smoke too much. You'll mess up your lungs."

Lotus raised a hand to acknowledge that she'd heard.

"You should quit!" Callie added.

Lotus didn't raise her hand a second time, either because she hadn't heard or because she had no intention of quitting. Callie sighed.

Their grandfather called Lotus his wild child. "Tougher to tame than a tiger," he often said. Callie had to admit that he was probably right.

Callie leaned over her Crock-Pot and scooped up the final sample of pulled pork in her spicy honey-barbeque sauce. She handed it to the teen boy who'd been waiting for it. When she turned back she found a group of three silver-haired women. They had clearly cut into the line, and there were murmurs over it.

"Oh, calm down," Mrs. Brinkman said to the disgruntled customers behind them. "Can't you see we're fixing to die soon? Do you want me to keel over standing in this line?" she demanded.

The collected people apparently did not want that since they made room for the geriatric mafia.

"Good morning," the ladies said as a chorus. Then they began discussing their options.

"Hold on, that's too many at once. She's just one girl here. Why are you all on your own with such a long line? Where are those sisters of yours?"

"I don't have any sisters. What can I get for you?" Callie asked, smiling.

They dithered a bit.

"I read about you girls. I know about your racket, dear," Mrs. Brinkman said.

"My racket?" Callie asked, raising her brows.

"Now don't get touchy. I won't say anything to Greg. You shouldn't either. He wouldn't go for that hocus-pocus play. The war turned him serious as a heart attack. Though plenty of my friends have survived those. Serious as a hand grenade, we'll say instead. Deadlier."

The people in line behind the Brinkman crew coughed and sighed, shifting on their impatient feet.

"What can I get for you?"

"Where are your free samples?" one of the ladies asked.

"All gone, I'm afraid."

"Well, how can I choose if there are no samples? You'll have to put out some more."

Oh, boy.

Callie smiled at her. "It is tough to choose. I'll tell you what. If you come back at one, I'll make you each a free sampler box. That way the next time you come you'll know just what you want to order."

"Oh, that's nice!" one said.

The other frowned. "Two hours? Now that's a long time. We'll just wait right here while you—"

"Not a chance," Mrs. Brinkman said, rapping the side of her cane against the table. "If you expect freebies, you'll wait for them. The girl is running a business, not a charity."

"But Phyl, I'm on a fixed income!"

"Aren't we all! Buck up. We've got a little pride left, haven't we? Move on," Mrs. Brinkman said, waving her posse aside. "I will be paying for my sampler box, and I will want a receipt. Two hours," she announced imperiously before walking away.

"Wow," Mrs. Koefer, the next customer, said, watching them go. "I can never decide who's scarier, Greg Brinkman who killed so many terrorists they gave him a medal or Phyllis Brinkman who I'm certain could take out a terrorist and all his closest neighbors with that cane."

Callie laughed. "I've only just met her and her grandson. Have you known them long?"

Mrs. Koefer nodded. "Greg went to Baines for elementary and middle school. I had him in class four or five times over the years. Smart boy, but got into a lot of fights, mostly with kids much older than he was. He must have been suspended a half-dozen times, but we always took him back, considering what he went through and living with Phyllis." Mrs. Koefer sighed. "How could you expect him to be anything but tough, you know?"

No, Callie didn't know, but she certainly wanted to. Why had Brink lived with his grandmother, and what had he been through? Had his parents died? She would have asked a lot more questions, but there was the line full of customers. For the first time, she was sorry her booth was so popular.

She went to work, filling orders. When she finally had a free moment almost two hours later, she put together the sampler boxes for the older ladies, who dropped by the booth just as she finished.

Mrs. Brinkman insisted on giving her a check for her sampler box of goodies. The amount was generous, and Callie tried to get her to void the check and write one for less, but Brink's grandma apparently had something to prove to her silver-haired set. Completely immovable, she would've made a good Marine herself. When they left with their boxes, Callie smiled and waved. They were cantankerous but charming in their own way.

When Callie had sold out of the majority of her wares, she closed her booth and transported her banner, tablecloth, and the empty bins to her van. A shadow passed over her, the clouds rolling in, which made her shiver. Her skin tingled, and she worked faster to load the van. The Melvilles were human lightning rods. She'd survived one storm strike but would never press her luck by being caught out in another rainstorm.

When she rounded the vehicle after closing the back door, she glanced at the passing cars, feeling uneasy. Then she froze. Inside a burgundy sedan that rolled by, she saw a face she recognized. The blond teenager rested an arm on the frame of the open window, her face tipped up to the sky. Callie's breath caught, and she leaned forward. The driver appeared to be a woman, but the cars leaving the event were too close together for Callie to see the make of the car or the license plate. She tapped her foot impatiently, craning her neck, trying to watch which way the car turned. She lost sight of it in the traffic and cursed.

The rain started, and Callie saw a streak of lightning. She gasped and immediately retreated into the van. It wasn't her lucky night though. She was only halfway home when the van began pulling to the right. She realized the tire that had been patched a couple months earlier must have gone flat again.

She pulled over and took a slow, deep breath, chewing on her lip and trying to calm herself. A bright bolt of lightning lit the sky, and she jerked her seatbelt off. By the time the thunder rumbled, shaking the earth, she was diving into the back. She landed on the rubber insulating mat and was completely still for a moment, catching her breath.

"I'm ok. It's safe here." She was lying on her stomach with the coolers and plastic bins looming over her. It took a few minutes for her to sit up and reach into the toolbox that was secured in the corner. She took out a flashlight and turned it on.

No problem, she thought, grimacing at her shaking hands. *It's gonna be fine. Roof over head. Butt on rubber mat. Nothing to worry about. The storm will pass. Until then, I'll wait it out.*

She opened one of the bins and took out a mini honey cake with oven-roasted pecans on top. She pulled out a paper plate and plastic knife. After cutting it, she took some sweat creamery butter from the cooler and spread it over the golden slice. She took a bite, the delicious rich flavors melting in her mouth, and she immediately felt better. She'd forgotten to eat, which happened a lot when she was busy.

She glanced at her phone, tempted to play some music, but she didn't want to run the battery down. What if the storm got bad enough to cause flooding? She might need to call for help.

Granger Falls didn't normally have issues with flooding, but the lakes and rivers occasionally overflowed. Callie doubted the water levels would get high enough for that at present, but you never knew what would happen where a Melville and a storm were concerned.

A bang on the back door made her jump, and she tipped her plate, spilling crumbs all over herself and the floor.

"Seriously?" she said when there was more banging. *No one but mermaids and salmon should be out in this weather.*

She realized it was probably some misguided person trying to come to her rescue. Or Lotus. Her cousin would know the risks of trying to save a Melville in a storm, but she'd try anyway. Sometimes Lotus was too brave for her own good. Callie lurched to her feet. If it was Lotus, Callie didn't want her out there one second longer than necessary. Way too dangerous.

She unlocked and opened the van's back door. Then she jerked back at the sight of the driving rain and the hulking figure standing outside.

"Hey, it's me," a familiar deep voice said.

"Uh, hi," she said, still inching backward.

"My grandmother and her crew passed by and saw you. She called and said you were stuck in the storm with a flat tire. Give me the key to unlock the spare on the back here. I'll change it for you."

Lightning backlit his giant shoulders.

Holy God!

She grabbed his forearm with both hands and tried to pull him inside. He was a two-ton boulder and therefore didn't budge an inch.

Thunder rocked the world. She let go, falling into the van and away from the open door.

"Get in or go away!" she yelled.

"It'll take me five minutes to change your flat."

"Are you crazy? No one's doing anything out there until the lightning's gone! Get in or go away!"

He climbed into the van and pulled the door shut. Water dripped from the brim of his baseball cap, and his soaked T shirt clung to his chest. It was slightly obscene and kind of delicious.

For God's sake, Callie! Possible kidnapper, etcetera!

Brink sat on one of the coolers, tipping his hat off and rubbing excess water from his face. He had indecently long lashes for a man. Totally unfair.

"She said you'd be afraid to be out in this storm. I didn't realize she knew you before yesterday."

"She didn't. She doesn't. Someone must have told her about my family."

"Your family? Something happened to them during a storm?"

"*A* storm? No. *Many* storms," Callie said, folding her legs under her and crossing her arms over her chest, trying to stay warm. "And actually no one is safe during electrical storms. You should never try to change a tire in the rain. Never mind that lightning could strike you at any second, a car could fail to see you and careen right into you."

"The speed limit here is thirty miles per hour, and in this rain, nobody's gonna be doing more than five or ten going down the street. It's Granger Falls, not Indianapolis."

Lightning struck something nearby, causing a deafening crack.

After catching her breath, she said, "Whatever. I still say I may have saved your life."

He grinned. "My hero."

"Precisely," she said saucily. "Hungry?"

"Definitely."

"Ham and jalapeño Havarti with honey mustard on kaiser rolls?"

"Yes."

"Good," she said, making them each a sandwich.

THE FOOD WAS GOOD. The company was better. Despite her damp clothes and surly lecture about the storm, the honey-wielding beekeeper looked edible herself. And whenever she shivered, his mind went to all the ways he might warm her up.

She was grilling him again with questions, which Brink

didn't mind. She was fairly smooth about it, looking at him with wide eyes and lowering her voice to make him lean in. He didn't doubt that her routine would put most guys in the mood to share secrets. Hell, it almost worked on him, and he wasn't most guys. He'd never been into pillow talk, even when there were pillows.

As if on cue, she unearthed a couple of large pillows that could've accommodated the half-horse of a mutt, Rufus. He wondered where the dog was. He hoped Rufus was coping all right with the storm. Not all animals did.

"Did you leave Rufus inside or out?"

"He'll be on the back porch. His pillow's on a rubber mat. He'll be ok." Her teeth caught her lower lip. "He might worry about me."

"About you?"

She ran a hand through the front of her hair, mussing it. "Right. I'm not sure if he can worry the way people do, but I know he's sensed that I freak out during thunderstorms. When I sit in the closet, he comes in and lies across my legs. He crushes them, but it's the thought that counts."

"What happened? To make you so afraid of storms?"

"I'm a human lightning rod."

"A human...lightning rod."

She rolled her eyes. "Do you think I don't know how crazy it sounds? And yet, eleven people in my extended family have been struck by lightning so far. *Eleven.*"

She paused, letting that number sink in.

He stared at her.

"Sometimes it kills us. Sometimes it—changes—us."

"What do you mean changes you?"

"It's a catalyst for a metaphysical shift. I have dreams that predict things that will happen. Nothing too specific. And I can't control it. But it's usually emotionally charged.

Once I start having one of those kinds of dreams, it doesn't stop until the event it predicts actually happens in real life. Then it's over."

He leaned back, studying her. She expected him to buy this? Then from the recesses of his memory something swam to the surface. An article, wasn't it? About a woman who claimed to have visions of lost children and then she conveniently found them. Upon skimming the feature, he'd speculated that the self-reported psychic somehow lured the kids away from home so she could miraculously save the day by discovering them in the nick of time. He figured it was a subtle con. What set of grateful parents and grandparents wouldn't want to reward a helpful citizen who rescued their precious little boy or girl?

"I think I read something about you once," he said.

She nodded. "In the newspaper. The old chief of police talked to a reporter for the *Kinley-Granger Falls Sentinel*. Word got around."

"So what's it like to be able to help a family that way?"

"Honestly, it's nerve-wracking and scary until it's over. If there's a rescue though, then it's amazing."

"The parents must be incredibly grateful."

"Yes, it's a huge relief for everyone."

"I'd imagine it is. Have there ever been times when the child isn't found?"

"It's not always a child." She took a breath in and shuddered.

She was either a really good actress or carrying out the searches had taken its toll.

"Not a child?"

"Sometimes it's a missing adult, usually a woman."

He leaned his shoulders back against the van's door. How would that work? He supposed adults could be tricked into leaving home, but then she would've had to have held them somewhere. His gaze slid over her. She was about five-five, a hundred and twenty pounds, not exactly imposing. Something else would have to be involved. A weapon or a male accomplice. Except wouldn't the victim who was reportedly lost eventually confess to being lured from home? The story might get distorted if it came from small kids, but there would be some commonalities, right?

"When the women are found, what do they say happened to them?" he asked.

She looked away.

"You don't always find them?"

"No, I do." She swallowed. "Eventually, I always find them. The dreams are relentless. There's no rest until they're found."

His muscles tightened. *Jesus.*

"But they're not always alive." She exhaled audibly. "The first couple of times I didn't know I was supposed to watch the news and be ready. I didn't realize what I was supposed to do. The first young woman was three hundred miles away. It took a while to discover where she was buried."

He rested his hands on his thighs. "You expect me to believe—"

"No, actually, I don't expect you to believe anything. You asked. I told you. End of story." She lurched up from the cushion, and he reflexively raised a hand, thinking she was going to come at him.

She cocked a brow. "Easy there, Riddick, I doubt I could take you in hand-to-hand."

He chuckled, but she didn't meet his gaze. She'd moved past him and flung the door open.

"No more light show. You are free to go."

He didn't move. "You're angry with me."

"I'm—it's been a long day. Please leave."

"Not until I change your tire."

"I don't need your help."

He fought it, but the corner of his mouth curved up. "All the same."

"Listen—"

"Not my turn to listen," he said, rising and exiting the van. "I made a promise to my granny. I can change the tire, or I can watch you change it, but I can't leave you on the side of the road in the middle of a storm with a flat tire. Will. Not. Do. It," he said.

She chewed the corner of her lip. His eyes zeroed in on that mouth of hers. He liked when she bit her lip. He would've liked it better if he'd been the one to do it.

"It'll be faster if I change it," he said, his attention returning to the flat. It was raining, which didn't matter to him, but she was trying to shield her head with her hands, which wasn't working out very well. And her hands shook, which he didn't like. It made him want to act, to get rid of that uneasiness, to make her feel safe again.

"Will you use a jack or just hold the car up with one arm while the other puts the spare on?"

He liked that she could joke despite being afraid. "It's a van, not a Fiat 500."

"Could you lift a Fiat?" she asked, eyeing him.

He grinned and winked. "Dunno. Never tried."

He searched for the gear to change the flat. When he'd been deployed in Afghanistan and Iraq, sitting on the side of a road without cover was a good way to get killed. What could be fixed was fixed immediately. The old habits died hard, which meant that procrastination never entered into things. Once he had the jack, he made quick work of the job.

"Wow. That was fast," she said as he stored the gear and flat tire.

"You know the spare is temporary, right? Don't drive on it at highway speeds. It's just to get you home and to a mechanic."

"I know." She shrugged. "Brink, I have two things to say."

"Shoot."

"First, thank you for helping me." Her voice was soft and sweet, and it drew out of him things that were neither.

"I owe you a favor."

"I don't want a favor," he murmured. "I will take a kiss." He slid an arm around her waist, pulling her to him.

It was a gamble that paid off.

She smelled like honey and pumpkin spice, and she kissed him like changing tires was just the beginning of the things he could do for her. He did not want to let her go, but when she pulled back he did.

She murmured something that sounded like "Bunny may have been a good kisser, too. I don't know."

"Who's Bunny?"

"Never mind."

"Good," he said, leaning close.

She put a hand up, and her fingertips landed on his lips. He bet those fingers of hers would taste good too, but didn't check.

"There were two things I planned to tell you," she said. "The first was that I owed you a favor, but that's been dealt with...sort of."

He smiled, not bothering to step back. She was inches from him with her fingers still on his mouth.

"The second thing is that whether or not I sleep with you one day is irrelevant."

He found that pretty damn relevant. And all the women

he'd known would have found it even more relevant than he did. She was odd in so many ways.

"Or it may be…if you turn out to be a bad guy."

He had no idea what she was talking about, but she smelled like honey and had blue eyes as big as saucers. He'd have talked conspiracy theories about Martians invading the moon if that's what it took to stay close to her. "Have you been with a lot of bad guys?"

"No, I avoid them."

"But you think I'm a bad guy?" he asked, trying to hold onto the thread of the conversation. Maybe she'd been hurt, and she was trying to tell him not to do that?

"Why do you need all those muscles anyway? What are you really planning to do with them?"

He grinned. "That really depends on the situation." A thousand hotter-than-hell scenarios fought to play themselves out in his head in an instant.

Her eyes never left his face as she took in a small breath. "Yes, well…look, don't take this the wrong way." She slid her hand around his neck and pulled herself up against him, her lips pressing hard against his.

In a single motion, his arms wrapped around her and lifted her from the ground. When she was sandwiched between him and the side of the van, he growled as he kissed her.

He would never know what they might have done if lightning hadn't hit the ground a few hundred feet away. It startled them both. He might have ignored it, but the honey-soaked lightning rod who was pressed against him dragged her mouth from his, saying, "Freaking storm."

He smirked.

"Put me down."

"You sure?"

"No," she said, looking harassed. "But I don't think we'll be able to enjoy ourselves properly if we're killed in the middle of things."

"I'll risk it."

It was her turn to smile. "Put me down," she said.

He eased her to the ground and let her go.

"You'd better not be a bad guy, Brink."

He held out his arms in surrender. "I'm a gym rat and arguably a badass Marine, but that's it. I'm not a bad guy."

"I hope not, for your sake."

"Why? What happens then?" he teased.

"We'll see," she said, unlocking her door before she looked back at him. "You're very strong and very tough. I admit that you're stronger than me, but not that you're tougher. We're equally tough."

"We are, huh?" he said, trying not to laugh.

"A hundred million volts of electricity ripped through me, and I survived. I dream of darkness that would make most people afraid to sleep. I don't fight it or try to numb my mind with anything. I face it. I'm tough."

Lightning struck a tree that was too close, and they both jerked again.

She yanked her door open. "I have to go, but I'll see you soon."

Before he could ask her the thing he wanted to know, namely when exactly he'd see her, she'd closed the door and started the van.

She pulled away from the curb, and he returned to his own car and watched her taillights disappear.

She was beautiful, strange, and probably crazy. He didn't normally do crazy. That never worked out long-term. Still, if he'd been able to, he wasn't sure that he would've changed a thing about Callie Melville.

8

As disturbing as the premonition dreams were, it was even more disturbing when she didn't have one. Usually once a recurring dream began, the frequency and detail intensified until the real event happened. And even though she couldn't control the dreams, it helped to know the pattern. Not only was the content of this latest premonition different, the stuttering frequency was unusual, leaving her feeling disoriented.

She stalked around the yard, dragging the hose behind her to water the plants that the sprinkler couldn't reach and muttered to Rufus, who kept his distance from her erratic spraying. She lowered the nozzle, which she had to admit she'd been wielding like a gun, and turned to her dog.

His ropey muscles tightened, ready to dart away if she raised the weapon. She sighed and shook her head.

"Ruf, I'm not planning to spray you. I'm just confused."

She glanced down and realized that she should've changed into a dress or shorts to walk around the flower beds. The bottoms of her peach pajama pants were blackened with dirt. She'd been distracted.

"Damn it."

She shoved a hand into her hair, but her progress was halted. She shook her head, regretting the absent-minded gesture which had snarled the front of her hair into a sagging puff. It had been in a loose, but neat braid until she'd started messing with it.

"The thing is, Rufus, no future dream last night. That's two nights in a row. What does that mean? Does it mean that Marine Man is the kidnapper and now that he and I kissed, he's distracted and putting his plans for the girl on hold? Or was he never going to be involved in any of this? Maybe I was just supposed to see his truck and find it to take me to the area where she lives." She glanced up at the sky thoughtfully. Could that have been it? And maybe the psychic dreams had slowed down because she was actively investigating. Maybe the universe wasn't harassing her to get ready because she was already on it and ahead of the game?

She tapped her foot. The wait was excruciating. She was attracted to Greg Brinkman. She wanted whatever was going to happen to happen already, so she'd know whether she was supposed to be kissing him or catching him.

"One thing's for sure. I can't just sit around waiting for more signs and clues. I have to *do* something!"

Rufus barked, probably more at her tone than because he had any idea what she was talking about. She raised a hand and waved for him to go play.

He bolted off.

"Don't wear yourself out!" she called. "When I get done here, I'm taking you for a walk. It may last all day, just so you know!" It was probably unethical to use her dog as cover, but the universe had given her premonitions and it had given her a dog. If they weren't supposed to be used together, they should've come with an instruction manual.

~

CALLIE AND RUFUS had been weaving up and down the streets near Brink's house for two hours, and though her dog would've kept walking, Callie's right pinky toe had developed a blister that rubbed against her sneaker with each step. She thought she'd had the shoes well broken in, but she guessed she'd never walked for hours in them. When it came to marathon walks, she was more of an amble down the street to a neighbor's, sit on a porch for cup of coffee, amble a few more houses down, stop at another neighbor's for a cup of tea, repeat. Technically she'd worn her tennis shoes for hours at time. She'd just never played tennis or anything else in them.

As she limped with each step, she had to admit the only reason she could keep pace with her dog was that he stopped every few feet for a scent check of the local trees and bushes. Could bark and shrubs really provide enough variety of smells to warrant such interest, she wondered irritably.

Then half a block down, she spotted a woman with long blond hair who was getting mail from her box. Her height and build were right, and she lived at the opposite end of Brink's block.

"This walk may have been worth the blister after all," she whispered.

Rufus of the dog hearing turned his head and cocked it.

Callie paused and watched as the woman went back inside. She needed to see her up close to determine if she were the girl from the dreams.

"C'mon, Ruf, let's have a closer look." Callie resumed her slow progress, glancing frequently at the house. She lifted her phone and took several photos of the house for reference. The woman didn't reappear, and Callie considered her options. She didn't have a good excuse to knock, and she really needed to take care of her toe. Yeah, she would come back later with a bandaged foot and a plan.

Her car was around a corner about a block away, but before she could reach it Rufus raised his head, catching the scent of something. He tore off down the block.

"Rufus!" she yelled, having no choice but to give chase.

Dog, I will kill you!

Rufus leapt onto a porch and barked loud enough to raise the dead. Squirrels fled up trees, and birds abandoned the yard in terror. Curtains in several windows jerked back. Callie did not make eye contact.

"Damn it, Rufus!" They were in Kinley, one town over from the threatening police chief, but that was no reason to push their luck with a complaint.

Callie grimaced at the pain in her foot, rushing as quickly as she could after her barking dog.

"Jeeze, Rufus! Quiet!" She hissed in frustration as the flaming pain in her toe shot up her leg. "Sorry!" she whispered as curtains fell back.

And was that porch attached to a house whose occupant she knew?

She was a few feet away when the front door opened, and the frame was filled with the enormous bulk of Greg Brinkman.

Bingo. "Of course. Just perfect," she muttered before forcing a smile and waving at Brink.

The screen door opened, and Brink bent to rub Rufus's head.

"Judas," Callie muttered under her breath when Rufus, who'd ignored her command to quiet down, stopped barking and licked Brink's hand.

Brink moved aside. Rufus strolled into the house like he lived there, and Callie thought maybe he should.

Unconcerned about the strange dog roaming around his house, Brink leaned against the doorframe, watching her approach.

"An entire town over to walk the mutt? What's that about?" he asked.

She flushed.

"You stalking me?" he asked.

"Yes," she said with more than a bit of menace. "Be afraid. Be very afraid."

He laughed.

She stood at end of the walkway. "You have thirty seconds to return my dog before he becomes your responsibility forever."

Brink turned his head and whistled. Rufus barked and appeared next to him.

Unbelievable!

And was that...? Yes, Rufus was chewing a piece of bacon.

"Don't you want to come in? Makes the stalking easier."

"I can't. I'm unarmed and injured. It goes against everything in the stalker handbook to interact with the prey on a day when I can't overpower him."

His smile widened. "Sure, because on most days you'd have no problem getting the upper hand." He walked onto his porch. He wore jeans and a blue T-shirt that was anything but plain as it stretched over that massive chest.

He came down the steps and joined her on the walkway. When he was a foot from her, he asked, "Injured how?"

"Very seriously injured."

"Stab wound?"

She nearly laughed, but managed not to. "Close." She

licked her lips. "Blister. Haven't seen it, but I'm pretty sure it's down to the bone."

"That is serious. You could lose a foot."

"I know."

Without warning he scooped her up.

"Hey!"

He carried her to the front door.

"Hey! I didn't agree to come in."

"Marine code. No man left behind."

"I wasn't being left. I was making my way home," she said, but trailed off when he carried her inside.

His living room was not what she'd expected. The walls were sage with gray accents. There were small trees in two corners and a stone fireplace with a shimmering painting of the ocean over the mantle. On another wall, there was a picture of a group of guys standing next to a tank. She would've examined the picture and the room more closely, but he carried her to a guest bathroom that was Spartan but immaculately clean. Even the snow white washcloths were rolled into uniform curls and stacked in a pyramid on the rungs of a polished, stainless steel stand.

He set her on her feet and said, "Strip."

"What?" Her heart thudded wildly because this could get really interesting, really quickly.

He banished the wolfish grin and said with mock seriousness, "Strip your foot. Let's see if we need to amputate."

She glared at him but sat on the edge of the tub and carefully removed her shoe. Blood had soaked the edge of her sock. She hissed in pain at the sight. Gingerly, she peeled off the sock, grateful the blood hadn't dried and stuck the fabric to her toe.

"Ouch," she said, looking at her foot. She'd rubbed her poor skin right off.

"In," he said, nodding to the tub.

She took him to mean she should put her foot under the tap to rinse it. She raised her pant leg and turned to rest her foot just under the tap. He reached over, but she batted his hand away.

"I can do it myself."

She turned the water on, testing the temperature with her hand until she was sure it wasn't too hot. She inched her foot under the water. The excess blood ran down the drain and cleansed the small wound.

She glanced over her shoulder to find herself alone. She returned to the task at hand and washed her foot with a cake of beige soap, glad it didn't sting as much as she'd expected.

"That's enough," he said.

She turned her head and found that he'd returned with First Aid supplies. He was pretty heavy-handed for a makeshift healer.

She turned and extended her foot. He caught it in a towel and patted it dry. There was something weirdly intimate about him handling her leg and injured foot. He dabbed some ointment on the toe, wrapped it with gauze, and taped the bandage in place. The whole operation took him less than a minute.

His efficiency was both impressive and annoying. Was there any physical task he wasn't an expert at?

He washed his hands and set the kit on an empty shelf. Everything neat and in its place. Military precision. She must be quite the wildcard for him.

"Close call," he said, "but I think you'll live."

She tried not to smile. "Maybe. If gangrene doesn't set in," she said solemnly. Then she added, "I noticed yesterday you have some battle scars of your own."

He nodded.

"What happened?"

"Combat."

"C'mon, don't you want to impress me with your war stories?"

He raised his brows.

"I assume you do. Otherwise you could've kept your shirt on yesterday, and I wouldn't have seen them."

"I took off the shirt to work. Not so you could see my scars."

"Hmm," she said with a skeptical sound. "Well, I did happen to see them."

"Of course you did. Stalker."

She laughed, and he finally let a smirk surface.

"Gonna tell me what happened?" she asked.

"Someday."

"Not today?"

"No."

"How about if I take a closer look and guess. You can tell me if I'm right."

He leaned against the doorway, looking amused. "Do I get to examine you, too?"

Heat rose in her cheeks, her heart thumping enthusiastically at the prospect. *Settle down. This banter is part of the investigation.*

"You did examine me," she said, wiggling her bandaged foot.

He stared at her until even that scrutiny started to feel sexy. She set her foot down and gave him a challenging stare of her own.

"No deal. That's a beautiful foot, but I haven't got a foot fetish, so it's not an even trade."

"What kind of fetishes do you have?" she asked.

The wolf grin was back. "None so far, but maybe you'll motivate me to develop some."

"Maybe so," Callie agreed, standing so she wouldn't have to crane her neck so far to look up at him. Standing barely helped. Boy, he was big. Was he that big everywhere? Could a guy be too big? More heat rushed to her face.

"What?" he asked.

She slapped her hands over her cheeks to cool and cover them. "None of your business."

"Bet it is," he said.

She took a deep breath in and pursed her lips to exhale. "I have to go. I have a lot of work to do today."

"Me, too."

"Good. I'll go then," she said, grabbing her shoe and sock.

"How far away are you parked?"

She frowned. She did not want to put the sock and shoe back on for the walk to her car, but she wasn't sure the bandage would make the trip if she went barefoot.

"I'll take you to it," he added.

"You're not carrying me to my car. What would the neighbors think?"

"I was planning to drive you, not carry you. And who cares what the neighbors think?"

"Oh, I see. You'll drive me," she said dismissively, though of course she did want him to drive her.

He grinned. "Did you *want* me to carry you again?"

"No, of course not. I was just trying to help you out."

"*You* were helping *me*?" he asked incredulously.

"Sure. You said you stay in shape so you can jump in and be a hero when needed. Without somebody to rescue, there's no need for you to spend all day at the gym. Today, I kept your muscles from being pointless."

He threw his head back and laughed.

"Excuse me. I need to get by. And Rufus and I would appreciate that ride to our car."

He didn't move aside. He reached overhead, resting his hands on the molding that framed the doorway. He effectively filled the space with his body. What the hell was his arm span? Twenty feet?

"From you, I don't take I-owe-you's, remember? If you want a ride, pay the toll."

"The toll," she said indignantly. "What toll? Another kiss?" As if she wouldn't love to kiss him again.

"For now."

She glared at him, but stepped forward, her heart thudding with excitement at the game. Were all tough Marines this much fun?

"You're too tall."

He locked eyes with her. "You'll manage."

"Bend down so I can reach."

He shook his head slowly, then inclined his head slightly, but not very much.

She realized his strategy and frowned. "My foot's injured, remember? You really expect me to go up on my tiptoes?"

"No pain, no gain."

"So you lied about not having kinks. You're a sadist."

He grinned, but bent forward. "Stop stalling. I want my kiss."

She wondered for a moment what Lotus would do to wipe a smirk off a cocky guy's face. Possibly stab him with the scissors from the First Aid kit. That would probably be taking the game a little far.

Callie stepped forward until her body was close enough to feel the heat of his. She laid her hands on his chest and pulled the fabric of his T-shirt into her fists. Then she rose onto her toes and leaned her entire weight against him so he had to tighten his muscles to anchor himself in place. If she had to work for the kiss, she wouldn't be alone.

She kissed him, softly at first, then harder. She teased his tongue with hers, right before she bit down on it.

He didn't yelp or draw back. He was too damn cool for that.

She pinched his tongue a little harder between her teeth. He let go of the overhead frame and grabbed her. He pulled her against him until she could barely breathe. She let go of his tongue, and it slid into her mouth.

By the time he released her, they were both breathing hard and she was a little dizzy.

When she swayed, his big calloused hands grabbed her upper arms to steady her.

"So," she said, blinking and trying to catch her breath. "Toll paid."

He studied her through partially lowered lids. "You bit me."

"Yes. You deserved it."

"Bite me again, and I'll give you what *you* deserve."

Promise? she thought. "If you can't handle the consequences, don't use extortion to get a kiss."

Whatever he said next was lost in Rufus's barking.

Brink looked over his shoulder. The dog pushed his muzzle into the doorway, growling.

"See. My dog doesn't appreciate your attitude either." She uncurled her fists, pleased by the stretched and crumpled fabric she left behind.

"The dog's jealous. Can't blame him. You used to be all his." Brink took a step back to let Rufus push his way into the bathroom. In the small space, Ruf nearly knocked her over.

"Easy," she said as the dog sniffed and then picked up the shoe she'd dropped.

"You should change that shirt," she told Brink. "It looks like your pecs have been fighting under there."

"Yeah, you stretched it out pretty good. We'll sort that out later." He glanced down at his watch.

"When later?" she asked.

"Tonight when I pick you up for our date."

"You didn't ask me out. I didn't say yes. No date has been arranged."

He just gave her a cool look. "Come on, move it, beautiful. You're making me late."

She glared at him. "Not my idea! I would've been long gone ten minutes ago if I hadn't had to barter for my freedom."

"Yeah, I could tell it was a real hardship for you by the way you had me wear you like desert gear, all hot and heavy," he said, waving for her to follow him.

He had not just said that!

She frowned. She didn't particularly want to leave. She wanted to argue. And kiss. And then argue. And possibly more than kiss.

In the end though, he drove her and Rufus to the car and dropped them off. Then he drove off faster than the speed limit allowed.

"Lawbreaker. Just as I suspected," she mumbled.

Unfortunately, Rufus's answering bark wasn't nearly as appealing as the banter she craved at the moment.

9

C allie skimmed the text from Brink again. He'd sent her a message that work would keep him tied up later than expected so he'd come by her place at eight-thirty. She texted back that she was impressed a man who got up at the crack of dawn could stay up as late as eight.

His response was *Thought a beekeeper would have to be sweet and mild mannered. How does someone like you keep from getting stung?*

She chuckled and texted back a winking emoji. Still smiling, she reminded herself that this shouldn't be all fun and flirting. If he wasn't coming by until eight-thirty, she had time to go on her fact-finding mission in his neighborhood. This time she'd park on the other end of the block. Her toe was fine, but not fit for long walks.

Around twilight, she put extra padding around her foot and slipped into loose clogs. She took Rufus back to Kinley.

Callie waited until there was no one around and then threw a doggie treat over the fence into the yard of the target house. She opened the gate, and Rufus went in obligingly.

She left the gate ajar and went to the front door and rang the bell.

No one answered. She rang again and waited, frowning. There was a car parked in front. She hoped it belonged to the homeowner.

Rufus barked, and Callie glanced at the side of the house, expecting him to emerge, but he didn't. She shook her head. No one was answering. She'd have to try again another time.

She walked to the gate and called Rufus's name. He didn't come, but he continued barking.

Her dog, it turned out, was not a good investigative wingman.

She pulled the gate open and entered the yard. Maybe there would be windows or a sliding glass door she could peek through to get a look at a photo of the blonde.

It turned out she would not have to work that hard. Standing on the deck was the blonde woman in question, and she had a gun pointed right at Rufus.

Callie gasped. "Wait!"

10

———

C allie hurried to get Rufus by the collar and to get in front of him to shield him.

"What is that dog doing in my yard?" the woman yelled. "I hate dogs! If he takes one more step, I'll shoot him!"

There were two things Callie noted immediately. The woman seemed hysterical and scared, and she looked like the girl from the dream about twenty years later.

Callie held up a hand. "We're going. He's not going to hurt you. He doesn't bite people. He never has. And I've got him anyway."

"You're not going anywhere. The police are on their way. You and that dog are staying right where you are."

"Oh my God, Mom! What's going on?" a voice asked from behind the woman.

"Stay back. Go inside."

"Mom, what are you doing?"

"There's a huge dog."

It was *her*. The girl from the dream was the gun-toting hysteric's daughter. She was dressed in an oversized T-shirt and sweats, with her long hair pulled through the back of a baseball cap, but there was no mistaking that pretty face.

"We found her," Callie whispered to Rufus. Then to the women, she said calmly and slowly, "I'm so sorry we came into your yard. We didn't mean to scare you." Callie knelt on the grass and tugged on Rufus's collar to get him to sit with her. "It's ok, boy. Sit still and be quiet."

Weirdly, the dog settled.

"Mom, it's ok. Put down the gun before someone gets hurt." To Callie, the young woman said, "I'm so sorry. My mom's deathly afraid of dogs. We were attacked in a park when I was little. She tried to fight the dog off and got bit. She thought it bit me too, and she's been scared of dogs ever since."

"Oh my God," Callie said, waves of guilt hitting her. The poor woman had post-traumatic stress from a dog attack, and Callie had sent a monstrous dog into their yard.

"I am so, so sorry," Callie murmured.

"I don't like dogs!" the older woman yelled, brandishing her pistol. "I'm going in." She spun on her heel and marched to the French doors. "And why are you dressed like that, Ash? You look like a lesbian truck driver, and you smell like a locker room."

Callie blinked, her jaw gaping open.

The young woman waited until her mother was safely inside. "I'm really sorry about the gun. She's had a little wine."

"It's no problem. I'm the one who's trespassing. Again, I'm sorry about my dog Rufus getting into your yard. I'm Callie, by the way. Callista Melville. Please tell your mom how sorry I am. And what's your name?"

"Ashleigh. Can you go now and take your dog? She won't calm down until he's gone and the gate's locked.

"Of course," Callie said. "Come on, Ruf."

Rufus rose and strutted out of the yard. Callie hustled after him and got him into the car.

She shook her head at herself. Pretty huge blunder, but at least she had a name and an address.

She put the car in gear and drove away with the adrenaline rush still singing through her veins. Rufus put his face out the open window and enjoyed the air blowing down his throat as his jaw hung open. Dogs' lives were much less complicated than people's.

"You know I joked today about being seriously wounded, but we very nearly just were."

Rufus was oblivious.

"Scary," she said soberly. She'd told Greg Brinkman that she was as tough as he was, but of course that wasn't true. The universe had almost bitten back to teach her a lesson. Was that how the universe worked? She wasn't sure. "You know what though?" she exclaimed, frowning.

Rufus, noting the tone, pulled his head in and looked at her.

"Maybe I shouldn't have gone around tempting fate by announcing how brave I am. But the universe could've given me a clue or two about the mother's being deathly afraid of dogs. I'm in bed sleeping for seven or eight hours. That's plenty of time to clue me in on that important point. I mean it's not just my safety at stake. You could've been killed. That's irresponsible of the universe."

She kept referring to the universe like it was a person, which she knew was odd. For the longest time though, it had felt like there was a sentient being behind the visions since she was supposed to act upon them. It wasn't some random extrasensory perception. Or at least not as her family understood it.

The dog barked, probably because he knew her pause was a cue that she wanted a response from him. Then he put his head out and went back to enjoying the car ride.

With effort, Callie loosened her clenched grip on the steering wheel.

No one got shot. And there's plenty of time to figure out if Ashleigh's in real danger and to prevent it. The mission is on track. Well, mostly on track.

UNDER NORMAL CIRCUMSTANCES Callie loved to get texts and voicemails. It was a testament to her closeness with her family and friends. And with her community. With 26,000 residents, Granger Falls was the perfect size in Callie's opinion. She loved that it had several family-owned restaurants, shops with quirky offerings, and vintage effacements on the main street.

This evening, however, all the closeness was making her claustrophobic. Mostly because she had done some things and was doing some things that she'd rather have kept secret. Before she'd even gotten home, the police chief had left a voicemail saying they needed to talk about her dog's recent visit to Kinley. *Seriously?* So sure, she and her dog had accidentally engaged in an act of terrorism, but she'd never expected word to travel faster than her car did on a fifteen-minute drive. She deleted the message. Maybe if she ignored it he'd forget about her.

In hindsight, Callie realized she probably shouldn't have told Ashleigh her name, or at least not her full name. But Callie had wanted to try to salvage the first meeting. She needed to be able to talk with Ashleigh again and to win her trust so she could convincingly warn her of the danger or at least keep an eye on the girl. So far...mission unaccomplished.

The next voicemail message was from Lotus, saying she'd be home if Callie wanted to come over. Because she didn't see Lotus as often as she wanted to, Callie normally never ignored an invitation from her. At the moment, however, Callie had other completely dangerous and inappropriate plans for the night. Callie texted that something had come up and the following night would be better.

She listened to her messages. There were a couple of business voicemails and then one from Natalie.

Natalie's message was casual, but they were as close as sisters and Callie knew that Nat was keeping tabs on her. Nat asked if Callie had made any progress on her investigation and whether she'd bumped into the suspected abductor again. Callie chewed on her bottom lip.

Now how do I respond to that? she thought. *Tell her I bumped into him on his front walkway and again in his bathroom? I really bumped into him there, lips and all.*

"If I don't call her back, she'll know something is up," Callie told Rufus as she let him out into the yard.

He took off.

She stood staring out back absently. "But if I call her back, she'll grill me, and I'll end up admitting that I'm kissing and going on dates with him. Then she'll *really* know what's up." Callie licked her lips. She needed to stop talking to herself.

Callie closed the door, shaking her head. She didn't have time to call Nat anyway. She needed to get ready. She'd been in the grass of a strange backyard, sweating in fear and hugging her smelly dog. Somehow, she doubted perfume manufacturers would be clamoring to create and bottle Eau de Rufus & Fear anytime soon. She needed a shower.

Callie hurried upstairs and got busy. She used a sea salt scrub that she'd gotten from a fellow artisan who lived near Santa Barbara. The friend incorporated bits of dried citrus in the mix, and it always left her skin feeling silky and her body refreshed.

After the shower, she massaged her skin with her Honey Buzz body lotion. Besides vanilla and honey, it had cloves and a touch of bitters to give it an edge to cut the sweetness.

She dried her hair and pinned the front up to show off her dangling amber earrings. She dug through her jewelry box to find the matching gold and amber anklet. She grimaced at the tangled mess in the box. It took ten minutes to unwind the ankle bracelet from its lovers. It was like a jewelry orgy in there.

One day she'd develop a better system for putting her jewelry away at the end of the night. Tossing it in a catchall container wasn't working out.

She slid into a hand-crocheted beige dress that she'd bought at a boutique in San Francisco. It made her happy to support local and regional business owners and artists. Except for her bra and panties, she was head-to-toe Pacific Northwest homegrown.

She couldn't find the shoes she wanted and had to step over dozens of overturned boxes and their spilled contents. Also, there was a really good lipstick color that would go with her makeup, but it wasn't in the vanity. Where had that gotten to? The bottom of her purse? A drawer in the kitchen when she'd cleaned out her bag?

The doorbell rang.

"No!"

He wasn't supposed to be early! Who'd trained him on dating etiquette? She raced out into the bedroom and looked at the clock. Eight-thirty precisely. Damn! So he wasn't early. He was exactly on time. Apparently, the military precision wasn't just for military maneuvers. Would she be able to break him of the habit of showing up on time? Or would he break her of the habit of running late? She really wanted to find out.

She hurried downstairs, the back of her hair flying wildly and making her think maybe she should've pinned it all up. She took a deep breath to compose herself and then opened the front door.

He wore a white shirt, unbuttoned at the throat, and dark trousers. He looked great and effortlessly cool. There was a white box under his arm.

"Evening," he said with a smile.

"You're early."

"No, I'm not," he said without even consulting his giant watch, which probably had twenty time zones and a missile launcher. Who wore watches anymore?

"You must be early because I'm not quite ready," she said sweetly, opening the screen door.

He stared at her. "You couldn't get any more beautiful, so whatever you have left to do can't be much."

She smiled. "For a man who spent most of his life making war not love, you're pretty good at this stuff."

"Just call 'em like I see 'em."

She drew him inside, glancing more than once at the white box. "There's a pair of shoes that's gone AWOL. I was tracking them down."

"Go ahead."

"Can I fix you something to drink? A cup of coffee? A glass of wine?"

"Nope."

"What do you have there?" she finally asked.

"A gift."

She nearly rubbed her hands together. Instead she waited. "May I have it now?" she asked. "Or do you require some form of payment first?"

He grinned. "I would really love to extract some form of payment from you, but then it wouldn't be a gift, would it?" He extended the box to her.

She took it and found it was heavier than expected. She hoped it wasn't food of some type. It wasn't that she didn't enjoy trying new jams and jellies, but it wouldn't be a particularly creative gift for her.

"It's heavy."

"Is it?"

"Well, not as heavy as a Fiat 500 I guess."

She sat on her coffee table, which was a reclaimed piece of petrified and heavily shellacked wood. She set the box on her lap and opened it. Inside there was a stunning antique lantern. The finish was a sort of whitewashed turquoise that had been distressed to let bits of metal peek through. The filigree work was beautiful.

"Oh, my gosh," she said, holding it aloft.

"You can put a candle inside, but if you like the style there are other possibilities too."

"What other possibilities?" she asked, springing to her feet. "Come with me. Let's see how it looks."

She went to the kitchen, found a pumpkin spice pillar candle and set it inside. She lit the candle and closed the lantern's door. Then she turned off the kitchen light and beamed, watching the intricate patterns of light flicker and dance across the stone top of the kitchen island.

She moved around the island to him, took his hands and rose onto tiptoes.

"I love it," she whispered.

He lowered his mouth to hers, and she kissed him.

"What other possibilities?" she asked.

"I can get more of those and string them together on a line. I'll cut a small trap door in the bottom of each for an outdoor bulb. For your yard."

"Oh!" she exclaimed softly. "Yes, that." She looked back at the lantern. "How many? Maybe I can get a few strings of them and crisscross them. Who made the lantern? How much are they a piece? I can call and arrange—"

He shook his head.

"What?"

"It's a gift."

"One is a gift. A really lovely and thoughtful gift. Strings of them are a home improvement project for which there needs to be a work order. What do you do, by the way, Brink?"

"I'm an electrical and solar engineer. I started in double-E but moved into solar energy a few years ago. I do project design that incorporates solar energy generation into the planning of new residential and commercial construction."

"You're Solaris Solutions, aren't you?"

"Yes."

"I hear you're kind of amazing."

He shrugged.

She wrinkled her nose. "Solar panels look so space age. It doesn't fit with the historic look and feel that we go for around here. But I heard you're pretty savvy about that and have suggested ways of positioning the panels so they're somewhat hidden. And that you have smaller panels that can be arranged in checkerboard patterns so they look less slapped on and more decorative on the roofs."

"Function can't be the only consideration. A house's curb appeal matters."

"I'd like to see your designs."

"All right."

"I didn't know you were creative. You don't seem very—"

"Flighty?" he teased.

She narrowed her eyes. "Just when I was starting to find you charming, you show your true colors." She flicked on the kitchen lights and blew out the pumpkin candle.

"Are you hungry? And how do you feel about venison?"

"Depends. Do I have to hear deer-hunting stories before it's served?"

"I won't have to tell you the stories. You'll be there. Deer-hunting is the first part of the date."

"Oh, my God."

"Rifles are in the truck."

"I prefer a shotgun," she said, barely able to keep from laughing out loud.

"Good to know. I'll make the adjustment when I take you boar hunting."

"I don't see why I should have to restrict myself to deer tonight. I say boars are fair game."

"Boars are strictly second or third date material."

"Who says? The hunter's guide to dating?"

"Yes."

Her next comeback died on her tongue when she realized that serial killers were hunters of human beings. Many of them also hunted animals for sport.

"What's wrong?" he asked.

"Nothing. Why?" she said, walking to the table and slipping her feet into a pair of sandals. She no longer cared about finding the crocheted heels that matched the dress.

"Sometimes you get this look, like someone walked over your grave."

"Lovely image. Have you considered writing poetry?"

He chuckled. "I think Byron's legacy is safe."

"You were joking just now about the hunting, right? You said you're not a hunter."

"Yeah, kidding. I don't hunt for meat unless you count the refrigerated section of the grocery store."

She picked up her purse, checking to be sure she had her keys and wallet. "Ready," she said, still feeling uneasy. Brink had hunted people. Terrorists. And he'd killed them. The fact that he didn't hunt animals didn't make him safe.

"Have you ever been to Mac's Pub?" he asked.

"Yes, but it's been awhile. I don't think we can make it there in time," she said, glancing at the clock. It was after nine already. "Their kitchen stops taking orders at nine-thirty."

"We'll make it."

"We can try," she said. "But I hope your backup plan isn't McDonald's because as far as I know that's the only thing over on the west side of Kinley that serves food after ten."

He smirked. "Have a little faith."

"I have a lot of faith. Faith that we're going to be eating burgers in your truck."

He opened the front door, and they were both forced to blink at the flashlight shining in their faces. On her porch, with his police cruiser blocking Brink's truck in, was the police chief.

"And now an unexpected delay," she murmured. "McDonald's it is."

11

For such a big guy, Brink moved like smoke. In an instant, his arm blocked her progress and pressed her backward to give himself room to step in front of her, which he did. He was so big, she couldn't even see around him.

It was so similar to what she'd done when Rufus was in danger that she had to smile. Except Greg Brinkman was much bigger than she was; he literally constituted a wall of flesh. Also, she didn't need a guy to intercede on her behalf. Unlike Rufus, she could speak for herself.

"Evening, officer," Brink said.

"It's chief, actually. Can you step aside, sir? I'm here to see Miss Melville."

Exactly.

"She's not armed or dangerous. You think maybe you can holster your weapon?"

Callie's jaw dropped. All she'd seen was the light and the cruiser. She hadn't realized Pell had his gun out.

"She has an aggressive dog. Where is he?"

"Locked in the yard."

"And who are you?"

"Brinkman. Greg."

"The Marine engineer?"

"Affirmative."

"Are you armed, Mr. Brinkman?"

"My weapon's in the truck."

Callie froze. He had a gun in the truck?

"Can you ask her whether the dog can enter the house without her letting it in?"

"There's no dog door on the back door. It has to be opened and closed for him to enter the residence."

How the hell had he noticed that? Who was he? Jason Bourne?

Callie folded her arms across her chest and glared at Brink's back. "If a certain mountain of muscle would take a step to the left or right, a girl could answer questions for herself."

She'd whispered, but she knew he'd heard her. He moved not one inch, not even to shift his massive weight.

"All right, the gun's away," the chief announced.

"Appreciate it," Brink said, opening the screen door for him.

"It's my house," she murmured furiously.

Brink had no right to invite a cop inside. Once they were inside you couldn't stop them from looking around. Not that she had anything to hide, other than the disastrous state of her closet, but that wasn't the point.

"Miss Melville," the chief said, removing his hat and putting it under his arm. He and Brink had matching, rigidly straight postures. It made her want to kneecap them both, just to see them hunch over.

"I tried to reach you earlier, but it appears you were busy," the new chief said.

"I still am busy. We were just leaving, hence our being at the door."

"I thought maybe you anticipated my arrival, your being psychic and all," he sneered.

Brink stiffened.

"The universe only shows me things that are important."

Brink gave her a sideways glance.

That's right. Anyone who jabs me gets jabbed back, police chief or not.

"I'm here to let you know that Kinley is mailing you a citation for failure to control your dog and for walking him without a leash. And to let you know Granger Falls's position which is: if that dog attacks anyone, not only will he be put down, you'll be arrested and charged."

"I understand," she said through clenched teeth.

"It's been suggested to the homeowner whose property you trespassed upon that she could sue you in civil court."

Callie's blood ran cold. She could certainly guess who'd been the one to suggest that. The police chief was on the offensive. She would have to watch her step. And Rufus's.

"If you really want your dog to have room to run for miles without a leash, you should consider moving out onto some farmland. There are acres for sale in a lot of other counties."

"We're trying to make a dinner reservation, chief. So you'll need to excuse us," she said, nodding at the door.

"Sure. I've said all I have to say to you. For tonight. Mr. Brinkman, you might want to ask around about the Melvilles. Every man who gets involved with one of these girls eventually regrets it. Or his family does."

What the hell! Had he investigated their family? Also it was a huge overstatement for this ass to say men regretted being with her or her cousins. There had been some accidents around Lotus, but in Callie's case, she'd been the one who'd been hurt.

Brink said nothing. He didn't take the bait and ask questions, but he also didn't defend his decision to date her.

You said you didn't need him defending you, she thought. While that was totally true, his silence still stung a little.

The chief gave a final nod and then turned and exited the house.

"There's certainly no way we'll make dinner at Mac's, and it is pretty late. Why don't we call it a night?" she said, trying to give him an easy out.

"Mac's a friend. He's holding the kitchen open for us."

"Oh. That's cool of him. Getting pretty late though for him to keep the kitchen open just for us. You could text and tell him that we're not coming."

"I could if we didn't want to go. Do you want to have dinner with me?"

She nodded. "But I'm not the one who has to be afraid. You heard Chief Pell."

"Vague talk about a woman being trouble? Maybe there are guys who could be scared off by that, but they're not career Marines." He held the front door open for her.

She stepped out into the cool and misty night, glancing up at the stars.

Brink pulled the door closed and made sure it was locked and secure.

"I'm not intentionally dangerous. None of us are. But things happen around us. Innocent people, some of them strong men, have been hurt or died under weird circumstances. We can be, I guess you could call it, unlucky for people."

"I'm not superstitious, Callie," he said as they went down the steps.

"You're not bulletproof either."

"You gonna shoot me?"

"I hope not."

He laughed. "Very reassuring. Get in the truck, Calamity Jane," he said, holding the passenger door open and extending his hand to help her inside.

"So you have a gun in here?" she asked, looking around. "Where? The glove box?"

"Like I'd tell you, stalker girl."

That made her smile and the tension eased some.

She waited for him to close the door and then opened the glove box. Just papers and a tin of mints. She found a safe in the console. It had a keypad and obviously required a code.

"In here, huh?" she said. "What's your birthday?" she asked, randomly pushing buttons.

"As if," he said, pushing her hand away and closing the top over the safe.

"What good does it do to have a gun locked in the truck? If the police chief had been a burglar, he could've shot us multiple times, and you couldn't have stopped him."

"Not a chance."

She tilted her head, eyeing him. "You really think you could've disarmed him before he got a shot off?"

"That's not what I said."

"You think you'd have had a good chance of stopping him even shot?"

"Probability is on my side."

"Maybe you have nine lives and you've used up eight of them," she countered.

He smiled. "You better hope not."

"Why?"

"Because that guy's gunning for your dog."

"You plan to stop anyone from shooting Rufus? Just so you know that might be a bigger job than you think. The chief wasn't even the first person today to pull a weapon on us."

"Are you serious?"

She nodded.

"What the hell did you do today that you haven't told me about?"

"This and that."

"Uh-huh. After dinner, we're going to have a long talk."

"Good. Because you still haven't told me how you got your scars. If you're going to be my dog's bodyguard, I need to hear your qualifications."

He laughed. "You're unbelievable."

"True." She smoothed down her dress. "And you don't know the half of it. The police chief is right. You should do some research, my dear."

"Or just ask for hazard pay. Think I need it?" he said.

She gave him a sideways glance. "You're so mercenary. I suppose it'll cost me more than a kiss if you get shot?"

"No. But if I get shot, I'll deserve more than one. And not necessarily on the mouth," he murmured.

She smirked. "Hmm. That's a crude innuendo, Mr. Brinkman. This is a date, you know. Not the barracks."

"Is it? Kinda hard to tell with all the talk of my getting shot."

It was her turn to laugh. "Whatever. You know meeting me was exactly what you needed to justify your lifestyle."

"Sure, of course. So my muscles won't be pointless."

"Exactly."

12

Most of the dining area of Mac's Pub had cleared, which made their corner booth seem intimate. They were at a large round table meant for a group, which Brink took advantage of by sitting next to her.

Mac came to greet them. He was dressed in jeans and a black T-shirt, with his blond hair escaping from under a bandana and curling haphazardly at the top of his neck. If a biker were crossed with the former member of a boy band, Mac would've been the result. On him, the look worked really well.

Callie and Mac got along immediately as he ribbed Brink in the way only a longtime friend could. She also pumped Mac for information, learning that they'd gone to high school together and that, not surprisingly, Brink had been an athlete.

When Callie asked about girlfriends, Mac let out a low whistle, shaking his head. "I'll let him tell you that story."

That story? she thought. Just one girlfriend in high school?

Callie had the venison with a fantastic maple bourbon cream sauce and roasted vegetables. Brink had venison stew that also smelled amazing. Callie thanked the staff profusely for extending the dinner hour for them, which made Brink smile. It was clear he knew everyone who worked there and considered them friends.

During dinner, Brink evaded most of her questions and countered with some of his own. She knew she couldn't expect to constantly grill him and then refuse to answer questions about herself, but it was tricky. Even with all the kissing and banter, she'd managed to keep some distance and perspective. When she talked about her family, though, it was like inviting him into her personal life. She wasn't comfortable having him that close.

"No, no sisters or brothers, but my extended family is tight-knit. Natalie's only a year younger than me. Lotus is a year older, and her brother is Nat's age. So the group of us grew up together. I swear during summers we stayed more at the big house, my grandparents' house, than we did at home. We had the pool and the lake and an enormous play-room. Plus, the golf course and tennis courts at the club. It was always so much fun to be there."

"Ever married?"

"Never married. Engaged once," she said, then rolled her eyes. He said nothing, and she felt compelled to add, "Everyone says we were too young, but that wasn't it. We met at the end of college, but the truth is I was the wrong girl for him. If I hadn't gotten the family gift-curse—I call it that because it seems to be both. Anyway, if I'd never changed from the girl my fiancé met, we'd have been fine."

"Maybe."

"Maybe," she said with a nod and a smile.

"People change a lot over the years. If he expected to be

married to the same woman his whole life, he should've waited to get engaged till he was sixty. Maybe later."

Her smile widened. "Are all marriages doomed then? Since you never know the person you're marrying?"

"No."

"You're not married, are you?" she asked, realizing suddenly that he could be. She thought he lived alone, but that might not be the whole story.

"No."

"Were you?"

He nodded.

"What happened?"

"Things changed. We lost faith in each other. I couldn't accept that as the new reality."

"You were the one to leave?" she said softly.

He nodded.

Callie sat back and folded her hands in her lap, falling silent. She was thirty-three, but she suddenly felt old and depressed. So many marriages failed. And wasn't it more likely to fail in a case like hers? She was frequently, and without warning, being dragged into unsettling and potentially dangerous situations. Who would want to live with that? Once it struck, the curse continued in most cases until death. She wondered if she could make the dreams go away with sleeping pills, then shuddered at the thought. No, no drugs.

But the dark, lonely thoughts lingered. She was unattached. So was Lotus. So was Nat.

"Tell me about this ability of yours."

She shook her head.

"Why not?"

"There's no point." She glanced absently at her dish. It had been so delicious. She wanted to concentrate on the meal and the fun she'd been having earlier. She didn't want to think about future relationships that might not survive.

Mac returned. "Chocolate flourless cake is all we've got left for dessert. It's really good. I know Brink won't go for it, but you should try it, Callie. I've got coffee or booze to go with it. What are you in the mood for?" he asked, looking at her.

"I'm good, actually. The venison in that cream sauce was amazing! The foraged mushrooms, too, really wonderful. Your pub has always had really good food, but that plate could hold its own against any in the state. Seriously, Mac. Awesome."

Mac grinned. "When you get done with this idiot, I'm gonna marry you." He winked at her, and she smiled back. Then he looked over her shoulder, and his smile disappeared. He held his arms out in a gesture of surrender. "I'm kidding, man."

She glanced at Brink, but she didn't see anything menacing in his expression. His face looked like it did when he wasn't smiling, which, albeit, suggested he might throw someone through a wall. But Brink's friend would've known that it was his resting badass face, right? So what had Mac seen the moment before she turned her head?

"I'll give you guys a minute to think about coffee and dessert," Mac said.

She turned her shoulders so she could see Brink more clearly. "You know it's ok to call things off quickly, right? I'm used to my premonitions being a deal-breaker. I'm still glad we met. If we hadn't, I might never have known about that maple bourbon sauce," she said, trying to add some lightness back to the mood.

"Glad you enjoyed it," he said, his tone so neutral he could've been Switzerland.

"Are you kidding me?" a hostile female voice said.

Callie jerked her head to look at the woman. It was Ashleigh's mother of the Rufus phobia.

"Problem, Heather?" Brink asked.

"Yeah, there's a problem. What are you doing with *her*?"

"Can't see how that's your business."

The woman's black mascara and eyeliner had feathered, making her look like a raccoon or a football player on game day trying to avoid the glare. The woman's cheeks were hotly flushed, and she'd clearly kept going with that wine Ashleigh had said she was drinking. Callie felt a small stab of guilt, wondering if Heather had kept drinking because she'd been scared to death by a certain doggie-mammoth.

"I'm really sorry about this afternoon. I'm Callie," she said, thrusting out a hand.

The startled and intoxicated Heather reached out, no doubt out of habit, before pulling her hand back instead of shaking Callie's. "You can give the perkiness a rest. Now I see what you were doing in our neighborhood," she said, her gaze shifting from Callie to Brink before finally settling back on Callie. "I better never see that dog again."

"I can't guarantee that, but I promise that you'll never have cause to be afraid. He doesn't like being on a leash, but he will be if I ever walk him in your neighborhood again."

"Not good enough!" she snapped, her voice too loud for the surroundings. "He got away from you once. He'll get away—"

"She said it won't happen again," Brink said in an even, low voice. "Move on, Heather."

Heather clucked her tongue. "Really? You're going to talk to me like that?" She glared at him. "And another thing, leave my daughter alone. I don't want her getting advice from you anymore, period. Got that?"

Brink just stared at her, unmoved.

"I asked if you got that?" she screeched. "Stay away from us."

Mac appeared and said sharply, "What the hell, Heather?"

She rounded on him and spewed anger, rambling about wild dogs and rude bartenders, jar-headed ex-jocks, and things Callie couldn't decipher.

"Unless you want to be barred for life, you'll lower your voice," Mac ground out, taking Heather's arm and pulling her away from the table.

Heather's voice didn't precisely lower, but her tone changed, more whiny than furious. When they were out of sight, Callie exhaled.

"She—"

"It's about that time," Brink said, sliding out the other side of the booth and extending a hand.

"We haven't gotten the check."

"It's all right," he said.

"Ok," she said, resting a hand in his and sliding from the booth. His hands were calloused and rough, like the rest of him she supposed. When she stood on the hardwood floor she slipped her hand from his, smoothing her dress, which had a tendency to bunch up.

He led her from the pub to the truck and put her in the passenger seat, like perfect manners were part of the Marine Corps code of conduct.

"She wouldn't happen to be your ex-wife, would she?" Callie asked.

"No," he said, shifting gears.

"You know her well though?"

"We went to school together. We dated a few times when

we were high school freshmen, before she moved on and so did I. We ran with the same crowd until I enlisted."

"I think there's something there. On her side at least. She's angry at me, and I don't blame her for that. But she seemed angry at you, too. And jealous."

He shrugged. "She's got no right to be."

She studied his profile. His strong jaw was set.

"She mentioned her daughter. Do you know Ashleigh well?"

"Well? No. She's a kid in the neighborhood."

He said nothing more. It was quite a contrast to the way he'd joked with her earlier. This surly muscle man was not a good communicator when annoyed. It didn't matter since they probably wouldn't be seeing each other again, but it bugged her anyway. She had really liked their verbal sparring and their flirting. It had been the most fun she'd had with a guy in a really long time, but she knew that even if he weren't a bad guy, she shouldn't get involved with him. He was too rigid. He'd given up on his marriage because he'd realized his wife wasn't what he wanted anymore. How likely would he be to put up with the Melville curse for the long haul?

The drive home was largely silent, except for the radio. He turned it on and told her she could change the station if she wanted. She didn't, so they listened to R&B mixed with rap on the drive. The combination of styles didn't blend particularly well on the tracks they heard, but there was something intriguing about the sound. It was like her and Brink.

She wanted to ask more about Ashleigh, but there wasn't an opening to talk about her. Or about anything.

When they reached her house, he delivered her to the front door.

"Thank you for the lantern and the really delicious dinner."

"You're welcome."

He obviously wasn't going to kiss her goodnight, so it was time for her to go inside, but her feet stayed firmly planted on the porch. He could've helped end the awkward moment by saying goodnight, but he didn't. He stood silently watching her.

"Well, I should probably go inside." She swallowed, shifted her weight, and finally frowned. "You could say something. Or you could go."

"If you want me to leave, go inside and close the door."

She smiled. "Is that part of the Marine Corps code? See your date safely inside the house at the end of the night?"

"It's not a Corps rule. It's mine."

"So if I stand here all night, you will too?" she challenged, the corners of her mouth curving up, feeling a little of that earlier chemistry.

"We wouldn't end up standing here all night. If what you're really asking is whether I believe I could outlast you in a standoff, the answer is yes."

She suppressed a smile. "You're so cocky. So sure of yourself. It's kind of an annoying characteristic of yours."

"I doubt that."

Her brows rose. "You don't think I know what annoys me and what doesn't?"

"Not if you claim my knowing my own mind does."

She was at a loss and stood silently thinking that over. Would she have rather that he was wishy-washy and unsure of himself? Hell no! She hated that. It had taken her ex-fiancé months and months to sort out whether he would give her up or keep her despite all her metaphysical brokenness. It had been the most excruciating emotional experience of her life. She'd been powerless to stop the premonitions, and she'd been powerless to make the guy she loved accept them. She'd just had to wait, and the longer she waited for him to make up his mind, the more her heart broke. She would never go through that again. If someone didn't like who she was, he could damn well move on with a helping shove from her to get him out the door.

The bad breakup had made every relationship since difficult. It wasn't easy for her to open herself up emotionally.

"You're right," she finally said. "Being decisive is a good characteristic, and it doesn't annoy me. It's just startling."

"Takes time to get used to something new."

"Can I ask you something?"

"You can ask me anything."

"Will you answer?" she countered.

"Probably."

"With more than one syllable?"

That made him smile. *Finally*, she thought. She hadn't realized how much she'd wanted to see him smile again until he did.

"I thought there was no point in my telling you about the premonition dreams I have. Do you agree that it's pointless?"

"No."

"Why not?"

"Why do you think?"

"Don't answer a question with a question. That really *is* annoying."

"I'm not sure what there is to say. You're either willing to take a chance or you're not."

"You said people change. Like your wife did. And you're not willing to accept those changes and do what it takes to make things work. The way I am is way more difficult to accept than a normal person's life changes. For a practical, regimented guy like you I would be a terrible girlfriend, even casually I can be chaos in a crocheted dress."

"You make a lot of assumptions. And you quit way too easily."

"You quit your marriage."

"Not before I tried like hell to save it."

"What if you do everything you can, and you still don't succeed? And the process is so awful...the absolute worst time of your life. Wouldn't you avoid that if you could?"

"No."

She stared up at him. "No?"

"Pain doesn't scare me."

She believed him. It wasn't some macho anthem. He was completely serious.

"Why not?"

"Because I'm used to getting through it and know I can. Listen, I had to fight that battle in my mind on other fronts a really long time ago. There were missions I went on that looked like they'd be one-way trips. We had to decide whether an objective was worth dying for. If it was, then we went. And sometimes guys were hurt or killed. I lost brothers on the battlefield that I still miss. But it comes down to one question: Are there things that are worth the risk? There are."

"Do you think I might be worth the risk?"

"I wouldn't be standing here if I didn't."

"But you could never believe that I have visions, could you? That I have psychic powers?"

"I don't know. There are things in the world I can't explain. I doubt that you're having visions of future events. I think it's probably coincidence and recall bias. But I don't think it's what I originally thought, which is that you're pretending to be psychic to con people out of money. That would be a deal-breaker. Are you a con artist, Callie?"

"No. It would actually be so much easier if I were. Then I could just stop whenever things got hard or inconvenient—which is most of the time."

"Have you ever taken money for helping people? There have to be rewards for finding missing kids. That would be an upside to being stuck with dark premonitions."

"You know, I considered it when I was younger. I felt justified. I mean I was dropping everything and working harder and longer hours sometimes than the police. But Lotus wouldn't let me. If she found out I took money for using the dreams to help someone, she'd lose it."

"Your cousin? Why?"

"She's convinced there would be terrible consequences."

"So she's superstitious, and you go along with that."

"I go along because I believe her. She knows things. Also, I never need money."

He raised his brows. "How's that?"

"Lotus always has money. If I run short and need supplies or anything, she pays. When I wanted to start my business, I wrote an entire business plan. Nat's got her MBA, and she helped. I had full-color Power Point slides, a great pitch, some collateral—though not enough really. The banks all said no, but not firm nos. They were impressed and gave me advice. I was working on my second business plan when Lotus got wind of the meetings. She was staying with a musician in the Everglades in Florida. I never found out how she heard. She just showed up at four in the morning one day with a duffle and told me to show her my business plan.

"I was shocked to see her, but she's Lotus, so there's

really no getting mad about the time of night. I gave my whole presentation in my pajamas. She never interrupted. She listened to every word and nodded at the end. Then she said I'd done a really good job and wondered if Nat had helped me. I told her yes, and she wanted to know why I hadn't asked for her help too, only Natalie's. Honestly it hadn't occurred to me to reach out to Lotus for something like that, and I told her so. She'd frowned and said if it was a question of helping me build my future, she didn't expect to be left out. She wanted to be a silent partner in my business. Then she gave me the duffle bag full of cash."

"Is she a drug dealer?"

"No. I think she wins it."

"That's convenient," he said skeptically.

"Not always."

"When is it not convenient to win money?"

"I think it's her gift-curse. She wins and makes money effortlessly. But people close to her have died. Natalie and I think there's a link. Lotus has never said so, but why would she be so adamant about my not taking money for using my gift?"

He said nothing.

After an awkward pause, she said, "It's okay to take off anytime. I know it's a lot to swallow."

"It's a lot to swallow," he agreed.

She stood very still, waiting for him to say something more, but again he left the night's end in her hands. She wasn't used to this. Men either pushed her to sleep with them and then pulled back and eventually left, or she pushed them away before they got the chance. There was never much time for her to stop and think.

"It's your turn," she whispered fiercely. "Tell me something personal. Tell me how you got those scars."

"Which do you want to hear? Something personal? Or how I got my scars? Because there was nothing personal about my getting the scars. I got them because I was an American Marine fighting terrorists. I was shot twice and stepped too close to an IED once."

"That was careless of you. What's an IED?"

He smiled. "An improvised explosive device. The IED took out a piece of flesh that was already scarred from bullet wounds and the blast injury missed my kidney by half an inch the docs said, so I decided I made out all right."

"Yes, lucky you," she said dryly. After a beat, she added more gently, "Did any of your friends get hurt that day?"

He nodded. "But none died. We all walked it off eventually."

"And you don't take that personally? Getting blown up?"

"They had to try to blow us up, Callie. We were coming for them. And as for planting IEDs that killed innocent people along with soldiers," he said with a shrug, "it wasn't the worst of what they did. Not by a long shot." He glanced away for a moment, staring at a distant horizon she would never see. "Evil men do evil things. I don't take it personally. I take it as a call of duty."

She crossed the distance between them and put her hands on his shoulders. "If you told that story that way to get me to kiss you, it worked." She pulled on him. "Come here."

13

The girl was a roller coaster ride, and they hadn't known each other two days yet.

Brink had been sure at the end of dinner that he'd blown it. He'd come off like an insensitive jerk by saying he'd written off his marriage, especially since he'd admitted it right after she'd said a guy she thought she'd spend the rest of her life with had headed for the hills rather than fight for her. It was probably the worst way he could've allowed the conversation to go. He'd wanted her to know there were things he wouldn't accept, but as soon as she'd withdrawn, he'd regretted not saying more. Women needed to hear certain things, like how they were different than a jealous and vindictive ex-wife. But because Callie was so beautiful and so sharp-witted he'd miscalculated, assuming she couldn't have been deeply hurt by some idiot guy in the past. And he'd still been concerned that the premonition story was some kind of ploy. He thought she needed a heads-up that he was a guy who could walk away when necessary, like if she turned out to be a con artist. Now though, he doubted she was a criminal. The idea she had that her family had some magical ability seemed more misguided than malicious.

But before he'd been able to get more information and make adjustments to get the night back on course, Mac, with spectacularly bad timing, had joked that when she realized Brink wasn't the right guy for her, he'd be happy to take his place. In that moment, Brink had wanted to knock out his closest friend. The sudden jealousy had blindsided Brink. He usually wasn't the jealous type. It had been part of the reason he'd never understood his ex-wife Mandy's irrational behavior. He hadn't been able to relate. He could now.

He would have to get a goddamned hold on himself. Jealousy was destructive as hell. He knew that firsthand. He wouldn't let it come between him and Mac, but for those few seconds when it hit him square in the chest, it had been like an IED going off.

He looked down at Callie now, her eyes half-closed, her lips slightly swollen from kissing him, and he felt himself going over a cliff into an abyss. She had told him the most bizarre, unbelievable things, but he just couldn't make himself pull back. He couldn't even make himself care. He wanted what he wanted. And he was looking at it.

"We've been out here long enough, beautiful. Invite me in or send me home."

She looked at him through long lashes. He held his breath.

"I should send you home."

But?

"But I don't want to." She licked her lips. "So come in."

Just like that, the roller coaster rose topside again.

∽

CALLIE LIT the pumpkin spice candle again and moved it to the living room where Brink's presence overpowered the couch. It wasn't a little couch meant for the petite people of the 19th Century, but he still seemed to take up a lot of space.

She'd kept the dimmer switch on the cut-glass chandelier low. She set the lantern in the middle of the coffee table. She doubted he cared about seeing it again, but she really did love it and wanted him to know.

"What can I get you to drink? Wine? Beer? Liquor? Soda?"

"Water."

She paused in the doorway. "I noticed you didn't drink with dinner. Is that because you don't drink alcohol at all?"

"I drink alcohol occasionally."

"But not tonight? Not with me?"

He shook his head.

"Why?"

He chuckled. "You know...I'd like to tell you why I'm not drinking tonight, but I'd better not."

She stopped and turned to stare at him. "Well, now you have to tell me. It would be bad manners to leave me dangling."

"I nearly got myself thrown out of your life tonight. I'm not looking to double down."

She walked back into the room and sat on the edge of the coffee table, facing the couch and him. He sat there with an arm casually resting across the top of the couch and practically reaching the other end. He wasn't the typical kind of handsome, and she was glad. It was how she knew his charisma was real, that their chemistry was real. Her attraction to him was like a heartbeat, thumping under her skin, palpable.

She leaned forward. "Let's see. You're a Marine, used to planning military operations. You wouldn't drink before one of those because you'd want to be sure your reflexes were sharp. On the other hand you could arguably be found at the top of Jack's beanstalk, so one beer isn't likely to dull your reflexes much at all. You could probably drink a six-pack and look fairly steady. So why not have a beer?"

He smirked.

She leaned further forward, and his eyes dropped for a second to the neckline of the dress. When they returned to her face, heat flooded her.

"It's a first date, but you think I'm kind of wild and unpredictable. So maybe we'll end up in bed together. And you worry that if you're drunk, you'll roll over and smother me."

He laughed, that deep rumble that she liked way too much.

"Come on," he said, shaking his head.

"It could happen. I bet you weigh almost as much as a tank."

"Come here," he said, holding out a hand.

"I am right here. I can't get much closer," she murmured.

"Yes, you can."

"Why should I?" she asked, really wishing she'd had a glass of wine because she suddenly did feel nervous. Not of what he'd do, but of what she might.

"Because otherwise my staying stone-cold sober will have been pointless, and I know how you like to help me justify my actions."

"Did you really?" she asked.

"Really what?"

"Stay sober in case we ended up in bed together?"

"I did."

"I think maybe you were so worried about my being a con artist because actually you're one."

He threw his head back and barked out a laugh. Then he stood up, leaned down and scooped her up like she weighed nothing at all.

"Closest bedroom, which way?"

"Halfway to the kitchen on the left."

He started to walk.

"Hang on. Take me back. I want my lantern."

"You're kidding, right?"

"No, Incredible Hulk, I'm not kidding. You can carry me three steps back to that coffee table."

He smirked but did as she bid him. Leaning forward suddenly, he made her gasp, but of course, he didn't drop her. Another good reason for him to stay sober, she decided. She reached out and caught the handle of the lantern.

"Anything else? Want to pick up some candles and a pack of matches from the kitchen?"

"Depends," she said sweetly. "How's your stamina?"

"Better than yours."

"Bet it's not."

"How much?" he asked, carrying her down the hall.

"Fifty—no, a hundred bucks."

"You're on."

14

H e was better in bed than any man had a right to be.

It was a ruthless combination of athleticism, knowledge of female anatomy and an almost preternatural understanding of her sexual fantasies.

By three in the morning, she was so sated and so sore, she had to stop him. She'd had four, possibly six orgasms by then. He'd had two she thought, but wasn't sure. He seemed always to be ready for more. She surmised that maybe he wasn't when he was using his hands and mouth on her, but she couldn't know since she'd been pinned down by those massive paws of his.

"Let me concentrate on you," she'd said breathlessly when she didn't think she could go another round herself.

He had had the good grace not to gloat. And she rewarded him for that by using her mouth on him with the kind of enthusiasm she usually reserved for consuming honey cakes. She thought vaguely as she fell asleep that she'd like to try tasting him drizzled in honey, too.

Sometime around dawn she woke, still boneless and

exhausted, to find herself alone. The candle had burned itself out, but taped to the lantern was a note.

Good morning, beautiful

She smiled. Apparently, he was good at many things, including notes. She went back to sleep.

Around noon, she woke to knocking at the front door. She wanted it to be the Hulk with lunch, preferably veggie tacos, which she was craving for some reason. She wrapped the blanket around herself, the tail trailing behind her as she got to the door.

She opened it to find Natalie with fluffy hair and an impatient expression.

"Hello, what day—time is it?"

"What daytime is it? Are you hung over?"

"Kind of," Callie murmured, wincing as she shuffled back toward the kitchen.

Was Brink even human? Maybe he was part werewolf. No, he was a Marine, so more likely he was the super strong mutant result of a government experiment gone terribly right. She definitely owed him a hundred dollars. She would have to pay up.

"What's wrong? Did you try Hip Hop Pilates again?"

"No," Callie said. Although, the night's workout had been a good one.

"Then what's up with you?"

"Nat, you know I can't talk before coffee. Why are you here?"

"You didn't call either of us back. And why haven't you had coffee yet? It's almost noon, Cal. And why...hey, is that the bedspread from the guest room?"

"Coffee," Callie murmured.

"It is, isn't it?" Natalie said, marching to the guest room door and flinging it open.

"Where is he? Did you make love to the serial killer?"

"He's not a serial killer."

"Oh my God!"

"He didn't choke me or hold a knife to my throat or anything of that nature." *But he did hold me down at times*, she thought, *which was sexier than I expected. And I did end up begging for mercy.* "Listen, I just wanted to get to know him—"

"In the Biblical sense?" Natalie exclaimed.

"And one thing led to another."

"Uh-huh."

"Listen, you weren't there. The man gets shot by terrorists while defending the free world, and he treats it like it's no big deal. Also, he carries me everywhere like I weigh less than a pistachio. And there was a bet. Plus, naked, he's like, I don't know, a gladiator. Special circumstances, Natalie. Special circumstances." Callie sighed. "Stop laughing, Nat."

"I can't help it. What the hell are you doing? You know if he's a bad guy and you don't stop him from doing something horrible, Lotus will show up and gut him to prove to the universe we're not shirking our duties."

Callie nodded, putting on the coffee. "Honestly, I'm not sure Lotus could take him."

Natalie gasped. It was a disloyal and practically blasphemous thing to say. They had discussed a long time ago that Lotus could probably kill a man with a paper clip.

"I don't care if he's a big bruiser of a guy."

"It's not just that," Callie said.

"Well, whatever it is, I sure hope he's not a bad guy."

"He's not."

"Sex made you sure, huh?"

"Kind of. Yes, pretty sure." *No woman-hating selfish sadistic serial killer gives a woman half a dozen orgasms and leaves her a 'good morning, beautiful' note,* Callie thought. Not that she'd known any serial killers or rapists personally, but she'd watched enough documentaries and movies to know thoughtfulness and sweetness weren't wired into them. Some faked it well, but she didn't believe anyone could've faked it that well. She knew she was biased. She and Brink had such amazing chemistry. She didn't want him to be the bad man she was hunting.

Callie checked her phone. There was a message from him.

Call me when you're awake.

She was awake, and she really wanted to call him. She glanced at Natalie.

"So, you've seen me. I'm not dead. Sorry I didn't call back. I didn't want you to feel complicit in case I decided to date the guy and he killed me."

"Very nice," Natalie said.

"And you're still welcome to help Lotus get revenge if he does. I'm not giving him a pass just because he's good in bed."

"Is he good in bed?"

Callie paused. "If sex were an Olympic sport, he'd be a gold medalist in every event."

"Wow."

"Now let me take a shower and have coffee. I have things to do today."

"Don't forget we have dinner with Gramps tonight."

"Oh, right."

"You forgot? You never forget! Who is this guy?"

"A mutant I think." Callie poured herself a cup of coffee and waved goodbye to Natalie, leaving her cousin to let herself out.

When Callie was upstairs in her room, she dropped the blanket and called Brink.

"Hello," he said.

"Hello." She paused. "How are you?"

"Good, now. Been waiting all morning to hear your voice. Then it turned into afternoon, and I wondered if I should send some paramedics over to resuscitate you."

"About that."

"Yeah?"

"You're freakishly good in bed."

He laughed.

"It's obvious you missed your calling. And when I pay you the one hundred dollars I owe, you will have taken money for sex, which will make you a gigolo."

He continued laughing.

"If you haven't thought yet about representation, I think I should be in charge of your career."

"Is that right?"

"Yes."

"Callista?"

"Yes?"

"I'm on a jobsite right now, so we'll have to finish this negotiation later."

"Okay."

"Hey," he said in a low voice.

"Yes?"

"I had a great time, too."

"Irrelevant."

He barked out a laugh. "Talk to you later."

She hung up and forced thoughts of the Incredible Hunk from her mind. She couldn't let herself get too distracted. If Brink wasn't the abductor then she needed to concentrate on finding the man who was.

She got online. It took her under five minutes to find Ashleigh's social media profiles. As Callie swigged her coffee, she reviewed the past year's worth of comments. There was nothing overtly threatening or creepy. There were plenty of men commenting on Ashleigh's posts, especially ones where she wore sexy outfits, but nothing raised any red flags.

Callie sighed and leaned back in her chair. She would have to start watching Ashleigh to see if anyone was stalking her in real life. She also made a list of the kids who seemed to be her closest friends. Maybe one of the girls had a dad or older brother who was obsessed with Ashleigh. They might be too smart to post openly on social media, but still be planning to take her. More neighborhood reconnaissance was in order.

15

Brink woke to persistent knocking. It took him a moment to realize it was eight at night rather than in the morning and he hadn't missed his workout. He'd crashed for three hours after getting home because he'd gotten so little sleep the night before. That thought brought a smile to his lips.

Callie was having dinner with her family, but that might be over. She could've been stopping by on her way home and was at his place. That would definitely make for another great night.

He rolled out of bed and strode to the front door. When he pulled it open though, it wasn't Callie on his front step.

Ashleigh's face was tear-marked with black mascara. She stood with clenched fists and a black skull cap over her long blond hair.

"Ashleigh, what are you doing here?"

"Can I come in?" she asked, shoving a hand up to wipe the moisture from her face.

He looked up and down the street. Heather wasn't

anywhere in sight. There were some people taking a walk about halfway down the block.

"It's not a good idea. What do you need?" he asked, rubbing the sleep from his eyes. He was shirtless and in shorts. He wasn't crazy about the idea of a letting a teen girl in his house when her mother had made it clear that he should keep his distance.

"I need to come in!" she whined. "Please?"

He sighed and took a step back. The kid rushed past him before he could change his mind.

"What happened? Why is she mad at you?" she demanded.

"Who? Your mom?"

"Yes, she said. "I'm not allowed to train with you anymore. What did you do?"

I lived my life, he thought. "Nothing that's any of her business. Or yours."

She sat on the couch and dropped her head into her hands, sobbing.

He stiffened. *What the hell?*

"I need help. I want to win this competition that's coming up. I can't—I just need your help. Is that too much to ask?" she said between crying.

"You don't need my help. Any of the gym staff can help you put together a—"

"Don't you even care? At all?" she yelled, jumping to her feet. "You're supposed to be this big hero with all your medals. I thought you cared about doing the right thing!"

"What is this?" he asked, taking a step back.

The doorbell rang, and Brink jerked to attention. Was that going to be Heather ready to lose her shit, too?

"Hey," Brink said sharply, talking to Ashleigh the way he

did to a soldier who was losing it during combat. "Calm down. Focus."

"If it's her, you can tell her to go away. She's drunk, and I'm not talking to her when she's drunk."

For Christ's sake, Brink thought irritably. This whole situation was like walking through an alley full of IEDs.

He pulled the door open and found Callie and a snarling Rufus at the door.

"Hi, let us in, so I can take him off the leash."

"Sure, yeah," Brink said absently, stepping aside.

She unleashed the dog, who bounded out of the room. A moment later there was a scream. Brink sprinted into the living room, but Ashleigh was all right. She was standing on his sofa, in her tennis shoes, yelling at Rufus whose teeth were bared.

"Rufus!" Callie said. "Come over here. Right now."

The dog growled, eyes still on the screaming girl.

Callie stalked forward and grabbed Rufus's collar. "Are you kidding me, dog? Let's go."

"Be careful," Brink said. He was sure that Rufus cared about Callie, but angry dogs didn't have perfect impulse control. "Let me—"

"No!" Callie snapped at the same time Rufus did.

Brink glared at the dog.

The dog glared back.

"Can you get her to stop screaming? He doesn't do well around raised voices." Then she went down on a knee, putting her face way too close to the dog's teeth. It took everything Brink had to not reach over and grab the dog's collar to yank him away from Callie.

Except when Callie spoke in a low voice to Rufus, the dog visibly calmed a little.

"What the hell is she doing here? What the hell is that dog doing here?" Ashleigh yelled.

"Hey," Brink barked. "Lower your voice."

"You're a fucking asshole," she screamed and then jumped down from the couch.

Callie literally flung her arms around Rufus to hold him in place as the girl tore past. Ashleigh slammed her way out of the house.

"Okay, Rufus, c'mon," she said softly. "Chill."

Rufus sat down, panting and looking around warily.

"How about a dish of water?" Callie asked.

Brink walked into his kitchen, filled a bowl and set it on the floor. Callie brought the dog, who walked over and drank, panting but at least not snarling.

"I think when he was a puppy people screamed at him while they beat him."

"It's going to be a problem if he bites someone. That police chief will throw the book at you."

"I know. I should've left him home, but he likes Gramps's house. And he liked you, so I thought he'd enjoy the visits."

"He acted like he wanted to take a piece out of me just now."

"He never goes after anyone. Just stands his ground and snarls. But I never let anyone near him when he's like that. Just in case."

"Except you. You got close to him."

"Well, if he's going to bite someone, it'd be best if it's me."

"Disagree. Strongly."

She petted the top of Rufus's head. "What are you talking about? He's my dog."

"Yeah, but you've got that beautiful face. If someone's

gonna get scarred up from restraining a dog, let's get the assignments right," he said, pointing at himself.

"That's very chivalrous of you. And also very sexist."

"Don't think of it that way. Think of it as you protecting your dog, because I guarantee if he'd bitten you in front of me, he and I would've had a serious problem."

"Don't threaten my dog. What was Ashleigh doing here?"

"Hell if I know. She woke me from a dead sleep."

Callie folded her arms across her chest and frowned at him. "No idea at all? That's strange, isn't it? You're obviously close enough friends for her to feel comfortable showing up unannounced."

"Not accurate. Don't get the wrong idea. She and I are not friends."

"I should go."

"No, you shouldn't," he said, pulling the fridge door open and taking out some leftover steak. "Hungry, Rufus?"

Rufus barked and walked right to him.

"Rufus, no!"

Brink dropped the steak onto the tile, and the dog went to work. "Good dog," Brink said, running a hand over the dog's back as he passed him.

"And you come with me," he said, catching her wrist and pulling her down the hall.

"Hey, stop pulling me. I don't want to be alone with you. I have questions."

"You don't need your dog to ask me questions."

"I might if I don't like your answers," she said.

"You're a little unhinged, you know that?"

"I'm not the only one. Why was Ashleigh crying? And why would she come here? And why aren't you dressed?"

"I told you. She woke me from a dead sleep by knocking on the door. I thought it was you, and I didn't want you to leave while I took the time to get dressed."

"Why was she crying?"

"Hell if I know," he said, closing the bedroom door so the dog wouldn't get jealous and butt in.

"Did you ask?"

"Didn't get the chance. You and Devil Dog got here right after she did," he said, pulling her up against him.

"Cut it out," she said, pulling away. "You should text her and ask her to come back."

"No, I shouldn't."

"Yes, teenagers can get so emotional they do irrational things. Let's make sure she's ok."

"She has a mother for that."

"Hey," she said, sidestepping toward the door.

He took a step forward, resting his hands on the wall on either side of her. "Checkmate."

"I'd like to know she's all right."

"Why?"

"Because I'm an irrational bleeding-heart female. Can you just humor me?"

"You don't sound like an irrational bleeding heart."

"Oh. Well," she said and then actually attempted to fake a sniffle.

"Try again," he said.

"Look, I don't know how to cry and act hysterical."

"Good," he said.

"But that Ashleigh girl's welfare is kind of my responsibility."

"What?" he asked, taking a step back.

"I can explain."

"Go ahead."

"I saw her in one of my premonition dreams. She's the reason I've been walking around your neighborhood. I was trying to find her. At first, I thought you might be part of the problem."

He took another step away from her. "Part of what problem?"

"I'm not sure. I think something is going to happen to her."

"And you thought I was the one who was going to do it?"

"I thought it was a possibility."

Shock became anger, and it grew exponentially as his mind raced. When they'd met, she'd asked him all those questions that first day not because she'd felt some big connection; she'd been milking him for information. And afterward, she hadn't come back to the neighborhood to see him. She'd been looking for Ashleigh. That's why she kept saying he'd better not be a bad guy. Callie hadn't been worried about him hurting her emotionally. She'd been worried he was a predator. She was spying on him and sizing him up as a suspect. *Fucking hell.* He'd been so far off base.

"I obviously don't think that anymore," she said.

"Lucky me," he said with a grimace. "But the girl's still the most important thing to you? Making sure *she's* ok?"

"I wouldn't say she's the most important thing, but yes, keeping her safe is important. I get those dreams for a reason. This is my chance to get in front of whatever's going to happen. You could really help me by—"

"No."

"Why not?"

"Because she's a teenager that's been trying to get close

to me, which was bad enough. Last night her mother told me in no uncertain terms to stay away from her. She told Ashleigh the same thing today. Then Ashleigh shows up uninvited, crying hysterically about not being able to see me. That is bad news from every angle."

"She has a crush on you?"

"Hell if I know. I want no part of whatever's going on. If her mother's getting drunk and she can't take it anymore, she can call someone in her family. Or talk to a teacher or school counselor. I don't want her coming to me."

"Why not?"

He wanted to bark, "Because people will get the wrong idea. Just like you did!" Instead, he kept himself in check. Callie had been using him. That would stop immediately. The slow burn in his gut flamed to fury. "You know what? It's time for you to go."

He pulled the bedroom door open and walked down the hall.

"What's going on?" she asked.

"Nothing's going on. Absolutely nothing. And that's the way I plan to keep it. You've got a reason for hanging around the neighborhood that's got nothing to do with me. Carry on, but leave me out of it."

"Are you telling me not to come back here to see you?"

"Yeah, that's what I'm telling you."

"I wasn't using you to get close to her. I didn't even know for sure that you knew her. If you don't want to help me make sure she's safe, that's fine, but don't just kick me out."

He was tired, and he needed to be alone to think. "You're complicated. I've had enough of complicated for one day."

The look on her face was worse than being shot. He'd hurt her. When would he learn that there were certain moments when he had to watch every goddamned word he said?

"Fair enough," she whispered and turned.

"Hang on," he said before he'd thought it through. He needed some distance, but it wasn't what he wanted. On a gut level he wanted to fight things out and then to keep seeing her.

"No, you've made yourself clear," she said, hustling toward the door.

"Callie." He caught her arm gently, but she yanked it away.

"Don't," she said.

Rufus, hot on their heels, let out of a low growl.

He half wished the dog would turn and attack him. At least if he'd had to defend himself against the dog, there would have been something physical to do. And most importantly she wouldn't walk out the door. They'd have time to figure things out. The way they had the night before.

With every step, that chance slipped away. He reached out, knowing he could stop her, but he stopped himself instead. Even though it went against every instinct he had. His heart hammered, and his muscles cramped, but he made himself stand still.

You're too wound up, and so is she. Let her go.

Within moments, she and Rufus were gone, but the anger and frustration didn't recede. He was restless. It felt worse than his first month of civilian life when emptiness threatened to swallow him.

He paced, counting breaths, slowing with each number. Then he went to the closet and got his bag.

When home doesn't feel like a home, go back to what you know, to what you can control.

Within the hour he was in the gym, gloved up and

hitting the heavy bag. He worked it until his muscles screamed and burned, and his mind was clear of everything, even her.

CALLIE UNDERSTOOD where Brink was coming from. She'd met him under false pretenses. One could argue that she'd dated him and slept with him under those false pretenses, too. He had every right to be angry and to pull back. No one could blame him for that. Except she did. She'd wanted him to understand and to not care that there were things in her life that were important enough to make her lie to a potential boyfriend.

She rubbed her eyes. She hadn't cried, but she'd been close. Standing in the kitchen, she traced patterns on the countertop with her fingertip. He had a right to his anger and confusion, but that didn't mean that she had to stand around and take it.

Never again, she'd sworn. She would not wait around in a soul-crushing depression for some guy to decide whether or not he wanted to be with her. She'd made a promise to herself, and she would keep it even if it killed her.

You're complicated. I've had enough of complicated.

So be it.

Safely in her own house, she did everything she could to distract herself. She cooked. She did yoga. She organized business receipts. She even cleaned her closet. And in between she petted Rufus who followed her from room to room. It helped to stay busy.

Finally she flung herself into bed and watched movies until her vision blurred, and she fell asleep.

The dreams were bloody and violent. She woke in a cold

sweat and rushed to the bathroom. She threw up until her stomach was so hollow she thought it might turn itself inside out if she was sick again.

She lay on the bathroom rug, too exhausted to move. Rufus lay down next to her and licked her sweaty face. It was gross but comforting.

"Something's wrong, Rufus. I better figure out how to fix it because I'm not sure I'll last long if I don't."

16

I t didn't take long for Callie to learn that one of the places where Brink and Ashleigh had been interacting was at a gym. After following Ashleigh there, Callie waited and returned in the afternoon to take a tour. On both trips, she'd filmed the cars in the parking lot to create a database of plate numbers.

After the tour, she joined, knowing it might be her best chance to interact with Ashleigh, since Callie obviously couldn't just show up at high school activities and hang around talking to students.

Callie quickly learned Brink had changed his routine. He'd normally worked out first thing in the morning, but following the night that both she and Ashleigh had shown up unexpectedly, "the big man" as he was referred to at the gym had started to split his workouts. Brink now did forty-five minutes in the morning and was out the door before Ashleigh arrived, then he returned in the evening for a second round after work.

It was also interesting that Ashleigh wasn't looking for him. The talkative guy at the counter had mentioned that

Brink and Ashleigh must have had a falling out. Before, Ashleigh had sought the big guy's opinion on everything and waited for him to spot her.

"Right after things changed, I asked where he was, and she says 'who cares?' She works out alone now and gets anyone who's around to spot her when she needs it."

This made Callie's job harder. It seemed like every guy in the place was friendly to women in the gym. They were quick to offer Callie advice, too. She tried to figure out if any of them were giving off a weird vibe, but they all seemed completely normal on the surface.

Callie attempted to befriend Ashleigh, but Ashleigh wanted nothing to do with Callie and went as far as to tell Callie to stop bothering her when she was trying to work out. Frustrated, Callie found herself in a holding pattern on that front. She'd wanted to get closer to Ashleigh so that she could either identify the threat or could warn Ashleigh effectively. With Ashleigh openly brushing her off, there seemed no practical way to advise her without appearing unhinged. Callie tried to stay hopeful about her chances of preventing Ashleigh from coming to harm.

Callie ran into Mac in the gym when she stayed late one morning. His blond handsomeness should've gotten her attention, but it didn't. None of the attractive guys interested her, except the one she never had the nerve to seek out.

"Hey, Callie, I didn't know you were a member here. Where's Brink?"

"He doesn't work out this time of day," she said, which was true enough.

"I know, but I figured he must be meeting you. No?"

"No."

"Oh," he said. "Well, have a good workout."

"Do a lot of the women he dates end up joining the same gym?"

After a brief pause, Mac said, "What women that he dates? You're first person he's dated seriously since his divorce."

"Who said we were serious?"

"His grandmother. And he brought you to my place at nine at night. It doesn't get any more serious than that."

She stared at him blankly.

"C'mon, you must know his routine. He's up before dawn every day for a two-hour workout. He eats dinner around five. No way he's waiting until nine for dinner for just anyone. Usually he'd be out cold by then. Plus, the way he was with you...if Mandy had seen that, she'd have scratched your eyes out."

"Who's Mandy?"

"His ex-wife. They got together in high school. Broke up for a while right after graduation. Her idea. Then she wanted him back. We went into the military. She was so paranoid. He was one of the few guys I knew who never cheated, but his wife was more jealous than anyone's. It was ironic as hell. She was relentless. Tracked down the woman he'd dated during the year they'd been broken up. Accused her of trying to get back in his life. It was crazy. She wanted to know where he was all the time. When we were deployed, she was sure he was with other women. Even when he was wounded. Lying in the hospital bed, he was supposed to be screwing the nurses, I guess. The guy really tried to work things out. Even went to couples' counseling, which he so did not want to do. Finally, Mandy cheated on him, calling it revenge. Honestly, I think she wanted him to kill the other guy. She chose a real prick that we all hated. I don't know what the hell was wrong with her. She even threatened to say—shit, it doesn't matter. When he filed for divorce, I threw him a party. It was about damn time. Hey, sorry, I know that's more than you wanted to hear. All I meant to say was that if she'd seen him look at you that night, she'd have finally had something to be jealous about."

She smiled. "Glad I met him after his divorce, for a lot of reasons."

He nodded, and they talked for another couple minutes before going their separate ways with a wave goodbye.

After the workout, she went home to do some beekeeping and gardening. When she finished, she went back to Brink's neighborhood, but took a detour down the block instead of waiting to be sure that Ashleigh made it home from school safely.

Callie couldn't take it anymore. She wanted to talk to Brink. She knocked on the door and waited. She could text him but didn't want to chance his saying he didn't want to see her. When he didn't answer, she knew he must not be home, so she sat on the steps reading a novel on her phone. She got totally engrossed in a tormented duchess's schemes to escape a mad duke, which is why she didn't hear Brink approach.

"You lost?"

She looked up. "I have been a bit. Not as much now that I realize how good it is to see you."

He rubbed a hand over his buzzed head and looked away, apparently undecided on how to respond. Would he send her away?

She waited a few moments, then said, "I think we've been out here long enough. You should either send me home or invite me in."

That drew his attention back to her. "Who'll feed your dog?"

"What do you mean?"

"If you come in, you're not likely to get back out."

"Ever? I knew you were a kidnapper," she murmured, hoping against hope that he'd let her lighten the mood, that he'd forgive her.

He shook his head and looked up at the sky. "I'm curious what I did to deserve this."

"Just lucky, I guess," Callie said softly. She stood and moved to give him a path to the door.

He unlocked it and held it open for her. She went into the kitchen, setting her purse and phone on the table.

"Someone told me that you eat dinner around five. It's a little early, but I could help you cook something."

He locked the front door. "No."

"Okay. Do you want to talk about—"

"No."

"Oh-kay."

He caught her hand in his and led her down the hall. He drew her into the bedroom and closed and locked the door.

"Brink, don't you live alone?"

"Yes."

"Who are you locking out?"

"Everyone in the world except you."

"Oh," she said and smiled.

He pulled his shirt off and then pinned her against the wall and kissed her till she was breathless.

"No talking? Just this?"

"If we talk first, things could go sideways. Let's start with the thing that can't go wrong."

There was a logic to his argument that she liked, but things had gone from zero to sixty so fast she was afraid she'd have whiplash.

"Hang on," she said, putting her fingers to his lips to stop him from kissing her again.

He stared down at her with those light-blue eyes, waiting. Finally he bit her fingertips and then let them go. "All right."

"We can talk?"

"Yeah. Let's do that in bed."

It would be crazy to go along with him. What if their conversation ended in a fight or a cold war? It would be a thousand times more awkward to have to get out the bed and dress before leaving the house.

He didn't give her a chance to object. He stripped down to his boxers and yanked back the charcoal bedspread to reveal dark red sheets.

"Wow. Who's your decorator? Dracula?"

"Sure." He lay on the bed and put his hands behind his head and waited. That body with all those incredible muscles...so hard to resist. Impossible, really.

Without giving it any more thought, she flicked off the light. There was still enough illumination coming through the curtains for her to see what she was doing. She stripped down to her underwear and crawled into bed. The sheets must have been six-hundred thread count because they were softer than any she'd ever felt.

"Dracula has very good taste."

"Thanks."

"I'm sorry I didn't tell you the truth about what I was doing in your neighborhood."

"It's all right. How could you have in the beginning?"

"It wouldn't have made sense to have told you right off the bat, but I should've told you before we slept together."

"Agreed. But I didn't need to take the lie personally."

"You didn't? How else were you supposed to take it? Sleeping together is personal."

"Exactly. A woman like you only sleeps with a man for one reason. She wants to. When I cooled off and thought things over, I knew you weren't just playing some angle. If you had been, you'd never have let me make love to you."

"If you realized that, why didn't you say so?"

"I did. Just now."

"You could've called me. Or texted. To tell me before now."

He didn't respond.

"You're still angry—or maybe not angry. But you're still wary that there's something in my life that could sometimes be a higher priority than you?"

"Not exactly."

"No?"

"Listen, if a kid fell into a pond, I wouldn't be jealous that you didn't make it home on time because you stopped to save him from drowning. I was angry because you misled me into thinking I was the reason you kept coming back to the neighborhood. And because you wanted me to text Ashleigh when that could put me in a dicey position. There was someone vindictive in my life once. I learned pretty quickly that you don't have to be guilty to be put through hell from being accused of things."

"But why would Ashleigh accuse you of anything? An angry ex-wife, sure. Maybe she would want a better divorce settlement, but why would a teenager falsely accuse someone?"

"Out of spite. I'm not saying it happens often, but there are some women who lash out when they don't get what they want. You saw her mother at the pub. That's the role model Ashleigh's got."

"But what is it that she wants from you that she's not getting? I take it she has a crush. Did anything ever happen?" She kept her tone neutral, but her body was rigid. Ashleigh was a very pretty girl.

"No. At first I just thought she wanted my attention. No dad around. She's known me a long time, like other kids in the neighborhood. But she was out of control when she was here. Way more than was warranted by the interactions we've had. That was completely irrational. I've never done more than spot her when she lifts and give her training advice when she asks for it. A few times over the years I cleaned out their gutters when I was doing my own and my grandmother's. I cut some tree limbs, too. Nothing major. Definitely nothing personal."

"Does the mother flirt with you?"

"On occasion."

"You don't flirt back?"

"No. If I wanted her, I'd have had her."

"And what about Ashleigh? Does she flirt?"

"She's tried different approaches to get attention. There were a couple of times when it seemed like she might be trying to flirt, but when I shut her down, she just tried something else."

"She's a really pretty girl."

"Yeah."

"Sounds like she wanted your attention badly. You could've slept with her."

"Probably."

"Were you tempted?"

"No. She ran through my sprinkler when she was five years old. I look at her and see a mixed-up kid who grew up without a dad. At the gym, I'm top dog—or one of them, so she gravitates to me. She doesn't seem to get that there are a dozen guys who would gladly quit in the middle of a workout just to count off her pushups."

"She knows that. I guarantee she knows it."

"Then why does she keep coming back to me? I don't encourage her. I never have."

"That's why. She wants to matter to the one she doesn't matter to."

"You saw something happen to her in the dream, what was it?"

"I'm not sure. I just see flashes of her. She's scared and in trouble."

"That I *will* help you with. If you call me and tell me who's going to try to hurt her, I'll make him rethink his plan."

"Deal," she said, feeling so much relief at hearing his responses about Ashleigh. She believed him. Everything she'd seen him do coincided with the things he said. Callie was convinced that he hadn't encouraged intimacy between himself and Ashleigh. Since a predator wouldn't discourage his prey from getting close, what she'd felt instinctively was logical too. Brink wasn't the guy from the premonitions.

She slid over and put a hand on his face to turn it. She kissed him slowly and then whispered, "Want to be done talking?"

He smiled and slid a hand over her belly and lower. "Let me show you what I want."

$\sim$

CALLIE WOKE at dawn to find Brink leaning over her.

"Are you all right?" he asked.

The dream came back in pieces. She'd seen his face. Not Brink's. Another man's. The one with Ashleigh.

"I'm okay," she said, catching her breath.

"What did you dream?" he asked, scrutinizing her.

"I think I saw him." She rubbed her eyes and then stared at the ceiling, trying to remember every detail. "He has brown hair with some gray. I'm not sure how old he is. Between thirty-five and forty-five I think. I only saw part of his face, and the visions were hazy and fragmented." She fell silent, thinking about the man's face and then thinking about the men she'd seen lately. "It wasn't anyone I've seen at the gym or around this neighbor.

"I didn't actually see him grab her either. He could be involved in some way that doesn't have to do with an abduction. Just like I saw your truck's license plate and the gazebo on Redwood Street. I think those pieces of information were leading me here so I could find her."

"You saw my truck, including the plate number?"

"Yes, your truck and part of the license plate."

"That's pretty—specific. And screwed up. Do you think this guy's going to use my truck to take her?"

"I don't know, but I doubt it. I've been in your truck. It doesn't look the same as the one that she's in."

"What's different?"

"I'm not sure. It just seems different to me."

"Is there anything you can do to increase your visibility during the dreams? Or to have the visions while you're awake, so you could tell me exactly what you see while you're seeing it?"

She shook her head and then smiled. "Thank you, though, for trying to help...for believing me."

"I don't know what I believe. Maybe it's just a random set of images that your mind cobbles together after the fact into something you think is a premonition, but maybe not."

She glanced at him, raising her brows at his intent expression. "What?"

"You said something in your sleep, something that's hard to buy as a coincidence."

"What was it?"

"Do I talk in my sleep?" he asked.

"I don't know. Both times I've slept next to you, I've been completely unconscious the whole time."

"No one's ever said so, but maybe I do. You might have heard me mumble something when you were half-asleep. But it's a stretch."

"I said something about you?"

"Yeah, something from my past. But I haven't thought about that time for years."

"What did I say?" she asked, catching his face in her hands. "Come on."

"I'll tell you later. We've got to get up."

"We do?" she said, shaking her head. "Maybe you do."

"We do. My granny knows you're here, and she expects me to bring you to breakfast."

"How does she know?"

"She's got more informants than the CIA."

Callie clucked her tongue. "I can't go to your grandmother's house looking like this."

"I know," he said, pulling the covers back.

"Hey," she complained, but she needed to get up anyway. She had investigating to do. She looked at the clock. It was still early to canvas neighborhoods. She had time for breakfast.

17

A s in all things physical, Brink was incredibly efficient. By the time she walked into the bathroom, he was already toweling off. His skin was cool and smelled like soap, which was way too appealing.

He wrapped the towel around his waist, but she blocked his exit.

"I think I'd like to inspect the troops," she said, running a finger over his flat abs.

He stared down at her. When she licked a bead of water from his chest, he grabbed her and lifted her. In one swift motion, she was over his shoulder and on her way back to his bed.

"Forget breakfast," he growled.

"No, we can't!"

"Sure we can," he said, pinning her down. "You started something. Let's finish it."

She laughed. "No, no! C'mon. I won't tease you anymore. Let me go."

He released her reluctantly.

She smiled and kissed him before going back to the master bathroom.

In the shower, she realized that there were no hair products. There was only a small cake of soap. She turned off the water and called out, "Brink, I need shampoo."

"Next time you stay over, it'll be there."

"There's none in the house right now? What do you use on your head? Soap?"

"Yeah."

"Seriously? I know you're a man, Brink. You don't have to prove it."

"You didn't mind me proving it last night."

She grinned, but called out with mock seriousness, "That was before I realized I couldn't detangle my bed head!"

PHYLLIS STOOD watch in the kitchen doorway as they cooked. "Let her have some room, Greg. Women don't want to be crowded in the kitchen."

"Yes, stop crowding me. I need room to bake," Callie said, trying to push him away from the stove. It didn't work.

"You gain the ground you can take, which in this case is none. You should make use of the ground you have, which is wherever I'm not standing," he murmured.

Callie took a step back. "I don't think Greg cares about homemade cinnamon rolls. I'll make them for you another day, Mrs. Brinkman."

"I could die today. Then what good will tomorrow's cinnamon rolls do me? Gregory, come away from there and let her have that oven."

"I'm making the bacon. You want cinnamon rolls instead of bacon?"

"I want you to act like a man and let Callista have the kitchen when she wants it."

"This is getting serious," Callie whispered. "She's never called me Callista before. I didn't even know she knew that was my name."

Brink hooked an arm around Callie's waist and moved her in front of him. In her ear, he whispered, "Don't burn the bacon, beautiful."

She smiled as he moved away.

"Now that there's a little woman to make us breakfast, I guess I'll man up and read the newspaper."

"Go ahead. Good riddance," Phyllis said.

Callie laughed and moved around the kitchen quickly. She was used to multitasking, so it actually was easier to do everything herself than to work with him in her way.

Phyllis cleared her throat. "It usually takes ten, sometimes fifteen years, to get them completely trained."

"Wow. Dogs don't take anywhere near as long."

"I've seen your dog, dear. I wouldn't brag about how well you trained him."

"Point taken."

"About my grandson."

"Yes?"

"His mother did everything for him. And then, because his parents died, I let him do whatever he wanted most of the time. His wife was a shrew and couldn't manage a tray of ice, let alone someone like that boy. The only one who showed him anything useful was the hussy."

"I beg your pardon?"

"Yes, I know about the hussy."

Callie didn't. She wasn't even sure what a hussy was. From the tone, maybe a slut?

"You know, Greg's wife was convinced he was unfaithful."

"I heard something about that."

"It was because someone turned him into a man in the sack and it wasn't Amanda. She was blind jealous, instead of just being glad he'd learned something. Now watch what you're doing, HoneySmacks, or you'll burn that bacon."

Callie, who'd been gaping, quickly removed the bacon from the heat and drained the grease.

"He doesn't think I know about Jennifer because they snuck around, but eighteen-year-old boys don't know how to hide what they're up to, not really. People see things, and they tell a grandmother the truth if they know what's good for them."

"How old was she?"

"Twenty-seven."

Callie gasped. "With an eighteen-year-old? That should be illegal. It almost was."

"Might have been. She met him when he was a senior in high school. Could've started before he turned eighteen. No way of knowing. He'll never say a word about it."

To his grandmother, definitely not.

"But anyway, I'm saying if you're smart you'll be patient. He's no doormat of course and never will be, but in the end, you'll get whatever you want from him if you handle him right."

"Mrs. Brinkman—"

"Now don't try to stop me from saying what I want to say. I'm not a young woman. I don't have time to wait around for you to ask for my advice."

"I wasn't going to try to stop you. Actually, I was going to say thank you. I know how much you adore him. I'm very flattered that you're happy about our being in a relationship and that you'd give me advice about him."

"Well, what other choice do I have when he's made up his mind?"

Callie laughed. "I wouldn't say he's made up his mind."

"No, you wouldn't. You couldn't. But I can because he's told me so."

Callie froze, nearly dropping the tray of hot cinnamon rolls.

"He told you what?"

"That I'd better be nice to you because when he marries you I'll want to see my great-grandchildren, and everyone knows the mother's in charge of where the children go and where they don't go. See how smart he is? Despite his useless wife, he's figured out plenty."

Callie's brows shot up. "He actually said that?"

"You'll need to cool those before you ice them, right? So we've got time, before I forget. Come in the living room."

Callie set the tray down with a clang, completely stunned, but she followed the tiny dictator into the living room.

Brink sat back on the couch, watching C-Span, which had maps of the Middle East that he was studying intently.

"That reminds me," Mrs. Brinkman said with a quick glance at the screen. "Spring break is coming up. You'd better go with these girls, Greg, so no one takes them."

"When did Iraq become a spring break destination?" Brink asked, not taking his eyes off the screen.

"Smart aleck. Girls get taken everywhere. Next thing you know they'll be sold online to a man in Saudi Arabia. Everything gets sold online these days, even girls."

Brink sighed. "She watched a show on human trafficking, so we're Threat Advisory Level Orange these days."

"Look at her. Big blue eyes. Skin light enough to freckle? And those sisters of hers are just as pretty. You can't let girls that pretty out of your sight these days. They get taken from a crowd, and you never see them again. And the men who take them get away with it. What can you do about it if you're here and she's there?"

Brink turned his attention to his grandmother. "Callie's not in high school or college. She doesn't go on spring break."

"Oh no? So how did I see her and her sisters in pictures on that Facebook? It should be called Face and Body Book if you ask me, if the girls are going to be in their swimsuits. You should have seen her in her blue bathing suit. It's a miracle she made it back from there. You'll be pushing your luck if you let them go alone. I'm telling you."

"We did go to the beach last spring. But it was a resort, Mrs. Brinkman. Kidnappers can't just walk onto the property."

"Oh, really? Because they follow the rules? Greg, you'll have to put your foot down."

Callie laughed until she saw the look on his face.

"Listen, we have someone with us who's almost as dangerous as your grandson. Her name is Lotus."

"The little girl who looks like Wednesday Addams?"

Callie burst out laughing. "Oh, my God. I wish I could tell her that you called her that."

"Well, what should I call her with that black hair and pale skin and her weighing even less than I do?"

"Um," Callie began, but she was at a loss.

"I've said what I needed to say. Don't fight him on this. If he's there, you can do whatever you want and never worry.

He saved whole villages in Iraq. The president sent me a letter. I'll be right back," his grandmother said before leaving the room.

"Wow. She's a lot to take all at once," Callie said, taking a look at the clock. She wanted to have finished breakfast by seven-thirty. "I need to ask you about something—" she began as Phyllis reappeared carrying a small bag. "In a minute."

"Now I know I should have talked this over with you first, Greg, but don't worry. If she doesn't like them, you'll get her whatever one she likes. But I know she buys used things. The girls call it vintage. So we should give her the choice."

"Gran, come on," Brink said, shaking his head.

Phyllis sat next to Callie on the couch and untied the ropes that held the pouch closed. She took out a plastic bag and flipped the pouch over, setting it on Callie's lap. Then she poured out a dozen gemstone and diamond rings onto the fabric. "You look. I'm going to ice the cinnamon rolls."

With a lap full of jewelry she looked over at Brink who was still staring at the ceiling.

"Looking for suggestions from the heavens? You may need to go outside for that."

"The only leverage that matters with her is great-grand-kids. I wanted her on her best behavior, so I suggested that she watch her step with you." He shook his head, smiling ruefully. "I should've thought about what would happen if she took the idea and ran with it."

"Wait, so you don't want to marry me after knowing me a few days?" she asked, looking through the rings. "But I'm pretty enough to be sold on the Internet. You better snap me up before white slavers do." Her smile faded as she thought about Ashleigh. Kinley and Granger Falls weren't sex-traf-ficking hubs, but Portland's international airport wasn't that far away. Maybe Callie needed to consider strangers as possible suspects too. Where might a random guy have spotted Ashleigh? A gas station near the interstate? A festival? A sporting event?

"Callie? You okay?" Brink asked.

"Yes, just thinking about Ashleigh for a minute. I've been checking out the routes between her house and the school during the main commute times, looking for men in trucks. I've also canvassed some of her friends' neighborhoods when they have their Facebook and Instagram settings set to private so I can't view pictures of their dads. I need to see as many guys in Ashleigh's circle as I can."

Brink stared at her, his expression grim.

"Yeah, not a cheerful subject. Sorry. Let me look at these," she said, forcing her attention to the jewelry in her lap. Many of the rings were gorgeous, but there was an opal ring that was especially pretty. "Are all these hers?"

"Some were hers. Some were passed down to her. That one was my mom's."

"Opals are so delicate. They're usually not a good choice for rings, but this one is really gorgeous."

"Put it on."

She slid it on her right ring finger, glancing down at the opal surrounded by small diamonds. "Beautiful."

"How's it fit?"

"A little snug. That's good for a ring though. Don't want it slipping off." She took it back off her finger and returned it to the collection. A moment later, she put them all back in the plastic baggie. She closed the ziplock carefully and returned it to the pouch.

"She started to tell me an interesting story," Callie said, setting the bag on an end table.

"Yeah?"

"About you and an older woman."

"An older woman?"

"When you were eighteen? A twenty-something named Jennifer?"

His brows rose, and he glanced toward the kitchen.

"Care to comment?"

"Not here."

"Okay. Let's wait on that. Back to the subject of the Ashleigh situation. A young guy probably isn't going to have the nerve, experience, or resources to kidnap a teenage girl. That's why I was looking more closely at guys in their thirties and forties that she'd met at the gym or who might have been watching her there."

He nodded.

"I've been thinking about what other older men have the opportunity to see and covet young girls. Her mother's boyfriends, the dads or stepdads of friends, male relatives, guys around the neighborhood, and school teachers. From what I've seen, she comes and goes from her house without ever interacting with the neighbors. They had your help with the gutters, so they don't have a go-to guy, right? There haven't been any guys who have been helping Ash and her mom out? Or a guy helping them financially? Maybe giving Ashleigh gifts?"

"How would I know? I can say that there's no guy coming over to mow the lawn or to fix things. I'd probably have noticed that. Besides teachers, you have to think about coaches, too. Kids spend a lot of unsupervised time with their team's coaching staff. I think Ashleigh is on a dance squad. Though, I'd expect that coach to be a woman."

"I'd like to get a look at her teachers. I wonder if there are any school functions or festivals coming up."

"No idea."

"So what did you think?" Phyllis asked, coming into the room with a plate piled with bacon and cinnamon rolls.

"They were all really pretty. I don't think we're ready to think about rings yet though."

"You can take your time, but don't wait too long. Country Club Ken and I won't live forever, you know."

"Country Club Ken? Is that your...boyfriend?"

She hooted. "No, your grandfather."

Callie laughed. "Oh, my God. That's hilarious."

"Isn't he the country club president?"

"You know, I think he is. He has to keep an eye on the golf club business. He's addicted."

"Didn't he get struck by lightning while playing golf?"

"Yeah, a long time ago. He's more careful now. Never plays in rain."

"Storms roll in quick," Phyllis said. "Lightning strikes fast, too. Like love. And snakes." His grandmother went back into the kitchen.

"Which of us has the eccentric family again?" Brink asked, shaking his head.

"At this point, I'm gonna call it a draw."

18

Callie had watched the main school routes, but hadn't seen anyone new who caught her eye. There was a back road with access to the school that was restricted to teachers and staff, but it required a key card and there was a security camera. It wasn't wide enough for her to park and watch the cars pass. She needed to work on a good excuse to get back there.

She'd been on the school's website, but for some reason there were no pictures of the teachers or staff. Only the principal and vice principal were featured with photographs. And the school's social media accounts were all set to private. Callie was sure that was meant to protect the students, but it was getting in *her* way of protecting a student. She stretched, knowing she had to concentrate a bit on her own life, too, or there'd be nothing left of it when she finished helping Ashleigh.

She went outside to check on Rufus. She always made sure she left enough food and water out for him when she planned to be gone for a while, and he liked staying outside when she wasn't home because there was plenty of space for him to run. She wondered whether he'd be lonely on his own if she started staying over at Brink's some nights.

Rufus bounded over at the sight of her, but after walking around the property with her while she worked and playing tug of war, he ran off to do his own thing. He was fairly independent, which worked out.

She refilled the bowls on the back porch and then left to make her deliveries. She decided to stop by Lotus's at the day's end, taking her boxes of food and pastries. Lotus answered the door wearing jeans and a Nina Simone T-shirt. Blues music wafted through the house's windows, which were all open, sheers blowing whichever way the wind went.

Lotus's guitar sat next to her piano, and Callie wondered if she'd been writing any new music.

"Did I interrupt you?" she said, nodding at the instruments.

"Nah. Had a jam session last night. Haven't gotten around to putting the guitar away."

"I'd love to come listen."

"We were just fooling around."

"Still," Callie said. "I'd really love to."

"Ok," Lotus said. "Want to play something?" Lotus pointed at the instruments.

They'd all had to take piano lessons. Lotus had gone on to learn guitar and trumpet, too. She had a surprisingly deep voice when she sang. It was one of the best parts of going on vacation as a trio. They usually got to hear Lotus sing during some impromptu set with a local band or at a karaoke bar.

"If I play, will you accompany me?" Callie asked.

"Sure," Lotus said, pressing a button to turn off the music that was playing. Lotus cleared papers from the stand so Callie could put up whatever sheet music she wanted to use.

"Or better yet. You could just solo something."

Lotus laughed. "You don't want to play?"

"I should definitely practice sometime, but not when I want to concentrate on listening to you."

Lotus shrugged and sat at the piano. She played a mix of songs, old and new, starting with "Brown-Eyed Girl" and a throaty rendition of "Shake It Off." Callie shouted out names of things she wanted to hear, and Lotus sang them. She finished with Nina Simone's "Don't Let Me Be Misunderstood."

When Lotus sat back from the piano, Callie couldn't help herself; she applauded. "You should be a rock star. Or a blues singer. Seriously, Lo."

Lotus just laughed. "So what's up with you, sugar doll? Why's Natalie worried?"

"Did Nat say she's worried?"

"She doesn't have to say it. She called to see if I'd talked to you. She said I should."

Callie took a breath and then let the whole story pour out. Night had fallen by the time she finished talking.

"What do you think?" Callie asked, her voice a little hoarse. She took a drink from a bottle of water Lotus handed her.

"About which part?"

Callie bit her lower lip. She really wanted to talk about Brink. Instead she said, "The girl. I thought about putting a GPS on her car so I won't have to constantly stake out their house to be sure she makes it home safely, but what good would that do? She's not going to be abducted in her own car. And I'll know by the dreams when whatever's going to happen happens."

"What about a GPS that she wears or carries? Something other than a phone because if the guy's not a moron that's the first thing he'll ditch when he's got her."

"She wouldn't take anything from me. Not even advice."

"What if your guy gave it to her as a peace offering?"

Your guy. She liked the sound of that. A lot. "I don't want to involve him. Like I said, he has reservations."

"Can't blame him. The world gets things wrong all the time. And she's underage. Messy for him if someone gets the wrong idea."

"I think his ex played games and accused him of things he didn't do. He's cagey about it. And just looking at him, he seems intimidating."

"Does he intimidate you?"

"No. He's in control of himself and doesn't seem to have anything to prove. He didn't take offense when I told him I'm as tough as he is."

Lotus laughed. "What did he say?"

"I don't remember. He probably laughed. He usually does when I'm being absurd. But I think he likes that I'm not afraid to tease him."

"Good men aren't afraid of strong women. Only insecure ones are."

"So you think it's ok that I've gotten involved with him? Even though I found him through one of those dreams?"

"He's not the guy. You've been on high alert. Your Spidey sense would've tingled by now if he was off."

"That's what I decided too." Callie's phone vibrated. She glanced at the text from Brink.

Are you coming here? Or am I coming there?

Callie smiled. "Speak of the devil. He wants—"

"Go. Bring him to Gramps's on Friday."

"To give your Spidey sense a shot at him?"

"Yeah."

"Okay." Callie stood and hugged her cousin. "Have fun tonight. And think about the rock star thing. I'd be a really good tambourine girl. I've always wanted to travel the world with a band."

"Since when?"

"Since I heard you sing the first time and thought everyone else in the world should, too."

Lotus shook her head. "Too dangerous." She hugged Callie tightly for a moment and then released her. "Call me if you need to. No matter what time it is."

"I will."

Lotus nodded and walked her to the door.

Outside, Callie leaned against her car and texted Brink.

Rufus is doing great. I'll come there.

Brink: *Good. When?*

Callie: *Now?*

Brink: *Yes*

Callie already had an overnight bag packed, so she went straight to his place, but she wasn't there long before banging on the door interrupted a conversation about dinner.

As usual, Brink moved swiftly to put himself between her and the door. When she took a step forward, he didn't look back, but his arm shot out to block her progress.

"Okay," she said softly. She'd only been planning to look around him but knowing that there really were dangerous forces at work, she didn't want to do anything to distract him.

When he opened the door, however, it wasn't an armed man. It wasn't a man at all.

"Is she here?" Heather yelled, trying to push her way in.

19

Brink stood in the doorway, blocking the woman's entry. "If you're asking about Ashleigh, no, she isn't here."

"I want to see for myself. Move. Just let me come inside," she said, trying unsuccessfully to move him.

"Calm down, and you can come in. Calm down!" he barked.

She seemed to visibly deflate, sagging against the bricks framing the doorway.

"We had a fight. I said some nasty things to her. I don't want to fight anymore. If she's here, just let me talk to her." She swayed unsteadily.

"Come on," Brink said, reaching for her. He bent and with an arm around her waist, he half lifted her, half supported her as he set her down on the tile floor.

The smell of stale wine and cigarettes filled the air.

"You're here again?" she spat when she spotted Callie.

Callie ignored the question. Was this it? Ashleigh's abduction? Callie didn't feel like it was. Usually when an event from a dream actually started, she had an adrenaline rush and a huge sense of urgency to get moving.

"I want my daughter. Ashleigh! Are you here?" Heather yelled.

"You start that, and you're out of here," Brink warned in an uncompromising tone.

"This is your fault. Why couldn't you just be nice to her? Would it have killed you?"

Brink seemed for a moment to be at a loss for words.

"He was nice," Callie countered. "As nice as it was prudent to be. Sit here. Brink, we should get her in a chair before she falls down."

Without ceremony, Brink propelled Heather into a kitchen chair, but he wasn't rough. The woman hung her head, staring at her hands.

"I never should have let her think...I just thought it would be better for her. He was such a jerk. You weren't."

"Who?" Brink asked.

"Back then at least, you were a decent guy. Not the asshole you are now. God, what happened to you?"

"War," he said.

"That's not true. You're nice to the other neighbors. You take care of that wicked granny of yours like she's made of glass. One little crack in her walkway and you're out there pouring cement. You've got time for everyone except the kid of one of your closest friends."

Brink frowned, shaking his head, but he didn't argue that Heather wasn't a close friend. They let her talk, mostly without interruption. Though a few times Callie or Brink tried to get some useful information out of her, like when the last time was that she'd seen Ashleigh and whether Heather knew of places Ash had gone in the past when she was upset.

To nearly every question that could've led to something useful, Heather said she didn't know. It was obvious that she spent most of her time absorbed in her own wine-soaked life.

Callie set coffee in front of her, offering her milk or sugar.

"What about honey? Haven't you filled his house with jars of your thousand-dollar honey yet?"

Thousand-dollar? What was she talking about?

When Heather began to cry, Brink took a marked step back. He even glanced at the door, like he was contemplating depositing Heather back outside on the front step.

"I know, I know. Marines don't cry," Callie whispered with a sympathetic smile.

"Neither do Brinkmans. Ask my grandmother."

"Better leave this to me then," she said.

"Good," he said, taking a post within arm's length from the table.

He stood at attention, and she had no doubt that if Heather tried to claw or scratch her, he would intervene in time. But of course, the distraught woman wasn't going to do either.

Callie pulled her chair closer to Heather's and rested her arms on the table, mirroring Heather's position.

"We're going to help you find her. Let's think for a minute. She's angry and upset. Which friends would she text? Which ones have families that are the nicest to her? Maybe someone whose parents work afternoon shifts so she could go over without having to deal with adults?"

Heather stared at the table, shaking her head. "I don't know. She's just...she drifted away from the other girls in her dance squad. She decided she wants to be a female bodybuilder. You can guess why," she snapped, throwing an accusing look at Brink. "Those women look so gross. She's so cute. Why would you want her to get all bulked up like that?"

"I've got nothing to do with her choices."

"Of course you do! That's all your gym is about. Bulking up. And she only went there because that's where you are. She could've joined a Planet Pilates or Anytime Fitness. No, she joins Iron Man."

"I don't get it either," Brink said with a shrug.

"She thinks he's her dad, doesn't she?" Callie asked.

Heather's eyes darted to Brink and then back down at her hands. "I never told her that. Not exactly."

"Are you kidding me?" Brink barked.

"You don't understand! I knew you wouldn't," Heather said, choking back a sob. "Did I ever ask you for anything? Did I ever ask you to do a damn thing?"

Brink clenched his jaws and his fists.

"But you had to know that he might say or do something that would hurt her feelings, since he didn't know that's what she thought," Callie said.

"I did. I worried about it."

"Then why would you let her think it?" he demanded. "Do you know how many times she tried to come over to hang out when she was young, and I turned her away? She wanted to come in and watch TV with me or to eat her lunch with me. If I'd been her dad...what kind of heartless dick says no to that? Jesus Christ, Heather!"

Tears welled in Heather's eyes and spilled over. "I told her you couldn't be around people very much. Because of something that happened when you were fighting terrorists. You needed peace and quiet or you'd get sick. She was little. She didn't question it."

"But why the hell would you—?"

"Because you were better than nothing! Which is what

Josh was! Nothing! He moved on and didn't want anything to do with us. He got married and had more kids. He's never wanted to see her. He didn't want me to have her. Can you believe that? The selfish prick! He's lived thirty miles from us her whole life and has never come to a single thing for her. Not one dance recital. Not one birthday party."

"Asshole," Brink said.

"You were gone a lot, but people talked about you, admired you. And when you were here, you were good with the kids in the neighborhood. You probably don't remember, but there were times when they were playing war or whatever and came to you to plan their battles. Remember? You'd stop working on your lawn and lean over their papers."

"It was nothing."

"And she came and asked you to let her enlist because the boys wouldn't let her play Marines with them. You told them there are women Marines. If she could pass the fitness test, she was in. So you made them all do jumping jacks and sit-ups and timed them climbing the fence. She was third fastest over the fence, even beating a couple of older kids. She was so proud of herself because she impressed you. 'I'm a Marine now. Just like him.' That's what she said."

"Jesus Christ." Brink said, clearly moved. He jerked the front door open and stalked outside.

Tears stung Callie's eyes, and she tried to blink them away.

"I know I shouldn't have," Heather said, clenching her fists. "I tried to tell her the truth so many times, but I just couldn't. She would've hated me. Plus, I thought it was a little good for her to have someone that she respected and was trying to impress. God knows she's ashamed of me and doesn't listen to what I tell her anymore."

"You were doing the best you could," Callie said before taking a big swig of coffee.

"I was!" Heather said through tears. Then she broke down, crying without restraint.

Callie put an arm around her shoulders and let her cry herself out. The coffee mug was empty by the time Heather finished.

"He's furious," Heather said.

"Don't worry about him. He'll be fine. He knows the difference between people doing the wrong thing for evil reasons and people doing the wrong thing for the right reasons. Let him calm down, and we'll—"

The door swung open, and Brink stepped inside. "Why didn't you tell me she left on foot?'

"I—what?"

"Your car's in front of the house. Did someone pick her up, or did she leave on foot?"

"I'm not sure."

Brink strode to the counter and grabbed his keys. "She could still be walking around. I'm gonna look. You all right here?" he asked Callie.

"Yes."

He nodded and went out again.

Forty minutes later, Heather got a response to the flood of calls and texts she'd sent Ashleigh.

Ashleigh's text read: *Ill b home by 7. friend will drop me off STOP calling*

Callie texted Brink to let him know that they'd heard from Ashleigh and that she was all right so far.

"I'll go. I want to be there when she gets home."

There was plenty of time for Heather to make the two-minute walk, so Callie suspected that in addition to wanting to be home for her daughter, Heather probably didn't want to be at Brink's when he got back.

Callie didn't comment. She said goodbye to Heather and saw her out. After, Callie washed the mugs and started dinner. Something simple, she decided, mixing a few spices into ground beef. She'd just found an indoor grill when the door opened.

Brink's face was a thundercloud. She dried her hands and leaned against the countertop, waiting.

"She's home. A girl dropped her off. Blue Lexus." He tossed his keys on the table and sat to take off his boots.

When he didn't speak further, Callie went back to making dinner. When upset, most of the people in her family were talkers. But her grandfather and Lotus were not. It had taken her a while to figure out how to handle them, but Callie had. She decided that Brink fell into the category of 'leave them alone for at least a couple hours unless they start talking first.'

He opened the fridge and closed it twice, clearly distracted. She had to force herself not to ask what he needed in there.

Finally, he dragged out some Brussels sprouts, tossing them on the counter like they'd been insubordinate. He put a hand on her hip and pressed, moving her over so he could get into a cabinet she'd been blocking. When he had the baking sheet he'd been after, he moved away.

He dumped the sprouts and doused them with balsamic dressing. He set the oven temperature and then wandered around.

"Rosemary roasted potatoes?" she asked, thinking he needed more to do.

He didn't answer, but ten minutes later, he had the potatoes washed and cut into quarters.

She formed the burgers while he threw the potatoes in a roasting pan and slid it to her. She added olive oil, onions, mushrooms, rosemary and sea salt. She raised the oven's temperature a bit and put the pan in.

When she turned back, he was staring at the ceiling, shaking his head.

"Fuck."

"Yep," she said softly.

"I don't want to talk about it," he said and then walked out of the kitchen.

"I know," she murmured and went back to what she was doing.

When dinner was ready and plated, she went in search of him. She found the lights on above the back deck. Brink was jumping rope. From the sweat soaking his shirt, she decided he might have been at it since she'd last seen him.

She opened the sliding door. "The food's hot now, but I can cover it with foil. Come when you're ready."

He stopped, tossing the rope aside. He panted, glancing around for a second before speaking. "I'm hungry, but I don't want to come in like this. Do me a favor and bring a plate out. I'll eat here," he said, nodding to the picnic table.

"No problem," she said.

She returned with his plate, plus silverware and napkins. Then she grabbed her plate and a couple condiments. When she returned, she found that he'd wiped the sweat from his face with the napkins.

"More napkins?" she said.

"No, you sit. I'll get them. And water."

"I can—"

"No, you sit."

She did so, and he went inside. She added a little ketchup and mustard to her plate, then waited.

He was back in moments with full glasses of water and a stack of napkins. He looked at the table, no doubt assessing it for missing items. Then he lowered himself to the bench and tore into the food.

They ate in silence. When she'd been younger, the lack of conversation and tension in the air would've unsettled her, but for some reason they didn't now. Probably because she knew what was on his mind, and in his place, she would've been overwhelmed by the revelation, too.

They finished and went inside, managing to take everything in with them in one trip thanks to his quick stacking and big hands. He made quick work of tossing things in the dishwasher.

"I'm lousy company right now, but if you can stand it, I want you to stay."

"I spent ten whole minutes packing an overnight bag. I wouldn't want all that effort to have been for nothing."

There was a ghost of a smile, which cheered her.

"I need a shower."

"So march to it. That'll give me a chance to poke around and snoop through all your stuff."

A brief smile that looked only half forced appeared for a moment. His arm snaked out and caught her. He pulled her to him and kissed her.

"Come with me," he said, pulling her.

She let herself be drawn down the hall and into the master bathroom. It was crowded with them both standing inside. It was a testament to the precision of his movements that he didn't bump into her when removing his clothes.

"Your clothes need a wash?" he asked, looking her over.

"No."

"Then why are you still wearing them?"

"Because I don't need a shower. I figured I was here for the show."

"I didn't drag you in here to be a spectator."

She studied him for a moment, understanding that he needed her close and needed another physical distraction from what he couldn't deal with yet mentally. She realized she wanted to stay close to him too. Without a word, she stripped out of her clothes.

20

The shower sex had been epic and just what he needed to take his mind off the fucked up situation with Heather. He didn't want to deal with it. Ever. But when he reached for Callie, she pushed his hands away.

"You're ready again? You should be in porn."

He rubbed a hand over his face. He was so glad she'd stayed. "Insatiable, my ex used to call me. She liked to prove she knew some five-dollar words."

"It's accurate, so we won't call a foul."

"The insatiable part was what had her convinced I must be screwing other women when I wasn't home."

"But you didn't?"

"No. Women are a luxury, not a necessity."

"Good to know."

She rolled onto her side to face him. "I can't imagine when you had time to shoot people if this was your normal routine."

He laughed softly. Her wisecracks made him feel better. It was like being back with the guys in his units. No matter how bad things got, when they made it back to base, there were the jokes and the endless ribbing. It was the way many of them coped with the stress of being in so many bloody firefights. He guessed he needed some levity from Callie, since his personal life was starting to feel like a hostile zone full of IEDs.

"This definitely wasn't my normal routine. Just taking advantage of the opportunity."

"For how long? Should I expect you to slack off on your gigolo duties in a week or two?"

He shrugged. "With your soft skin? Nah. I'd imagine I'll probably cut back to twice a night in a year or two."

"Acceptable."

He chuckled.

"I expect certain things out of this relationship. It's on you to make up for all those orgasms I've been missing out on for so many years."

"The ex-fiancé didn't deliver in that department?" he asked, wondering how the hell it was so easy to talk about past lovers with her. He normally shut down every conversation about his ex and any girlfriends' ex-boyfriends.

"Well, I don't have a lot of comparative experience, but I never had a really great time in bed with him. What was the name of that older woman again? Jennifer? Maybe she can put on a course."

"She wanted me for one thing. And for that, I will be forever grateful."

"Me too."

He laughed again.

She yawned and curled deeper into the covers.

"You tired, sweetheart?" he asked.

"Yeah. You?"

"Yeah, really tired."

She laid her hand on his face, and like so much about her, it was sweet and satisfying.

"Thanks for not pushing earlier. I appreciate that you left me alone when I said I didn't want to talk."

"You're welcome."

He'd seen the look on her face when he'd come in from searching for Ashleigh. He'd expected her to launch into a never-ending conversation that would've just wound him tighter. But unlike every other woman he'd ever been with, she'd seemed to get that he felt like slamming his fist into the wall and talking had zero chance of making that feeling go away. How the hell had she known to just leave him be? Maybe there was something to that claim she made about having psychic powers.

"Can I ask you something?" she asked.

Damn. He was so tired. Maybe he'd spoken too soon about her understanding him.

"Shoot."

"Are you afraid of the dark?"

"What?"

"If not, can we skip the night lights? I like it totally dark when I'm trying to sleep."

His ex-wife had bought those, but he sure as hell wasn't going to tell her that. "Those are so you won't bang into the walls if you need to find the bathroom in the middle of the night."

"I'll risk it."

He got up and yanked the night lights out of the sockets and tossed them on the dresser. The room was pitch black.

"Better?"

"Mmm-hmm."

He climbed back into bed. "I lied to you today," he said,

thinking if she didn't take that bait she'd have to give up her woman card.

"Bad Hulk. Superheroes don't tell lies. Work on that."

Unreal, he thought, closing his eyes.

"Lied about what?" she asked.

He grinned. *Gotcha.*

"I said I wasn't serious when I told Granny I was going to marry you."

"So you were serious? But you didn't admit it because you thought you'd seem like a lunatic if you admitted it to me?"

"I thought it might spook you."

"I don't spook, Hulk. I told you. I'm tougher than you."

"Good to know." He waited, but she was quiet, and for once that wasn't what he needed. "How about it? The plan to eventually get married...sound about right to you?"

"I haven't ruled it out," she said lightly. "The universe is pulling for you. That's a big deal for a Melville."

He didn't know what she meant, but at the moment he didn't care. He rolled over, pulled open the drawer of the nightstand and felt around for the ring. He found it and fished it out. Brink rolled back, finding her arm in the dark and following it down to her hand. He slid the ring over her knuckles, settling it in place on her finger.

"Is that the opal?"

"Yes."

"How?"

"Got it before we left. In case you wanted to try it on again."

"You're a lunatic, but you're a clever one."

She fell silent, and he held his breath, but he would've taken a bullet before admitting it.

"I probably will end up marrying you. It's just the sort of thing I'd do."

There was probably some romantic thing he should've said, but he had no idea what it was. Instead, he found her hand again and held it.

21

C allie had gone to Granger Falls High School, but she'd been to Kinley High a few times for sporting events. Kinley hadn't been maintained as diligently as Granger Falls with its constant coats of fresh paint and updates, but the fifty-year-old Kinley buildings were in good repair.

Callie had debated telling Heather about her premonitions and consulting her about the best way to approach talking to Ashleigh about them. But on the whole, she agreed with Brink. Heather was irrational and often drunk. She wasn't a person Callie wanted to consult with about delicate conversations, especially ones that involved psychic powers.

In the end, Callie had decided things were still too tense for her to approach Ashleigh. Also, Heather still needed to tell Ashleigh that she'd been lying about Brink. It didn't seem prudent to hit the girl with another big revelation. *Oh, by the way, I'm sort of psychic and you're in danger...don't know when or where or by whom, but be ready.* Too much. Way too much for anyone to handle, let alone an emotional teenage girl with a chaotic home life.

Callie smoothed down her blue suit and straightened her pearls. Since she was taking stock of herself, she glanced for the millionth time at the opal-and-diamond ring that she was still wearing.

She and Brink hadn't mentioned it again, but he'd glanced at her hand that morning and smiled upon seeing it. Without a word, he'd kissed her goodbye. She hadn't told him of her plans to go to Ashleigh's high school. The situation was complicated enough for him. If she discovered something important, she would share it later.

Her cover story was that her daughter was going to switch schools and Callie was trying to decide where to put her. Although she'd been heavy-handed with her make-up, she could tell the administrative assistant who was taking her on the school tour thought she looked very young to have a fourteen-year-old.

As they walked down corridors, Callie tried to peer through the windows, but it would've looked very strange for her to pause to check out individual rooms. She stopped when asking questions to slow the tour down. She wanted to be in the hallway when classes ended, which would give her a better chance at passing open doors and seeing teachers.

She stopped at each trophy case to ask about athletic programs and to examine the photographs. She wished the school's website had a full picture roster of the teachers and coaches, but it didn't so here she was going old school on the investigative front.

The assistant tried to hurry her so they'd be clear of the hall by the final bell. Callie asked if she could meet her back in the office, citing the call of nature. Even with her guide saying she could use the office's restroom, Callie shook her head and ducked into the girls' bathroom at the end of the hall, calling over her shoulder that she'd be right out.

When she heard the final bell, she exited the stall, washed her hands and made her way back out. She went against the flow of teen traffic, looking in each class as she went. At one point she spotted Ashleigh, who saw her as well. The girl's eyes narrowed.

Time to go, Callie thought. She turned and strode down the hallway quickly, still trying to glance around for a look at the teachers. She saw several men, but none who looked like the guy she'd seen in her dream.

She poked her head into the office. "I've got a text and need to go. Thank you so much for the tour. I'll be in touch!" She didn't wait around to say goodbye to the principal. It felt imperative that she get away immediately.

By the time she crossed the visitor's lot, she was practically running. She got into her car and shoved the key into the ignition. When she'd pulled out of her space, it was nerve-wracking to have to line up in the rows of exiting cars. Maybe it hadn't been so smart to wait for that final bell.

She didn't stop hyperventilating until she was off school property and halfway home.

"No harm, no foul," she murmured when she was safely in her driveway.

She went inside, her pulse gradually returning to normal. She still needed a way to see all the teachers and coaches.

Inside the house, she couldn't settle. On and off a feeling of uneasiness hit her. Was time running out? Would the abduction happen tonight?

She fed Rufus and put in him the yard for a while. Then

she shoved her keys, her cell, and her wallet in her pockets so she'd be ready to go out at a moment's notice.

Two hours later while she was doing Internet research, trying to match social media profiles to Kinley teachers, the doorbell rang.

Her heart rate kicked up, and her skin tingled. She licked her numb lips and contemplated ignoring the bell, but she couldn't really expect to get away with that. The lights were on, and her van was out front.

She walked to the front door, took a breath, and pulled it open. As she had expected, the police chief stood in the doorway.

"Hello, chief," she said, impressed that she'd managed to keep her voice steady.

"Step outside, please."

"Why?"

He waved for her to join him on the porch. She was gratified to see that his gun was safely in its holster.

"Outside now."

She stepped out, pulling the door closed behind her.

"Callista Melville, you're under arrest. You have the right to remain silent..."

She'd known something was about to happen. She'd thought it would be the Ashleigh abduction, but apparently it was her own impending arrest that she'd been feeling. *Just great.*

Now that it was happening, though, she guessed she should've been a little relieved that the waiting was over. Unfortunately, it was hard to feel relieved when he slapped handcuffs on her wrists. This was not good.

"Really? Handcuffs?" she balked.

He ignored her, walking her down her porch steps with

a firm grip on her upper arm. The chief put her in the back of his cruiser and then slid behind the wheel.

Through the metal grate, he gave her a satisfied expression. "I warned you. You've got no one to blame but yourself."

She rested back against the seat, counting the slow deep breaths she took in and out. It was the way she always calmed herself down when she woke from a nightmare. Except this time, she was the person in trouble and she had no idea how she was going to rescue herself.

22

C allie thought she held it together pretty well for her first time being booked. Except for the part where they fingerprinted her, and she almost cried, she'd been as composed as an upper-middle-class former spelling bee champ could be expected to be.

In the interrogation room, she'd kept her composure, too, at least outwardly. She said she wouldn't answer questions without her lawyer and asked for a phone call. That made the police chief turn surly, and she was taken to a holding cell.

That went all right except for the delinquent who was even more surly than the chief and who tried to pick a fight over the gum she wanted that Callie didn't have. Then the girl took exception to Callie's looking in her general direction. She was obviously looking for an excuse for a confrontation, and Callie was getting tired of trying to calm her down.

"Stop looking at me!" the girl said.

"I wasn't. Can you stop being a pain in the ass? I'm having a lousy night, too."

"You bitch!" the girl snapped.

Callie had been ready, but the girl was fast with her fists. Before slamming into the wall, her fist banged the corner of Callie's mouth.

The guys across the row started yelling and cheering them on. Callie didn't throw punches, but she did shove her shoulder in the girl's chest which knocked her down. Before the girl could get to her feet, officers filled the hall and unlocked the cell.

"I tripped! I tripped!" the girl screamed as they hauled her out of the cell.

Callie wiped the blood from the corner of her mouth with her sleeve. She could feel her lip swelling, but the cut was shallow and her teeth were fine. Most of the punch had been delivered to the cement wall.

The girl cradled her arm. "I think my hand's broken. Hey, stop. I need to go to the ER. I need to go now."

They put the girl in another cell, leaving Callie alone. She sat on the cot.

"What happened? She attacked you?" a cop asked Callie.

"I'm okay."

"You shouldn't let her get away with it. You want to talk to the chief about—?"

"No, I just want a phone call or a lawyer. Nothing else."

"Suit yourself," one of them mumbled.

They left her in the cell for two hours. When she was given her phone call, she called her grandfather.

"Hi, Grandpa. It's Callie. I'm in jail. I got in trouble working on family business. Can you send a lawyer?"

"Which jail?" he demanded.

"Granger Falls."

"What idiot would arrest you?"

"The police chief."

"I'll be right there."

"No, Gramps, please don't come. Just send the lawyer. I'll explain everything at dinner next time. But could you call Lotus? Not Natalie. Lotus will stay calm, but Nat will get worried and worked up."

"What about you? How are you doing?"

"Just fine."

"Good girl. Stay calm."

"I have to go now. Talk to you soon. Love you." She ended the call and let them lead her back to her cell.

Thirty minutes later, she was in a room talking to a tall middle-aged lawyer in a decent suit. His bowtie gave her pause. It was a little too...old-fashioned? Sweet? She needed a pit bull of a lawyer. She needed a Rufus of a lawyer.

Her lawyer, who looked like he should've been advertising kettle corn, explained that she was accused of stalking a teenage girl. Then he asked whether it had anything to do with the lightning strike.

She nodded. "I was watching over her and trying to find a criminal that's in her midst."

"The girl took pictures of you sitting in your car, watching her house. The school said you solicited a tour under false pretenses?"

"I did. Had to."

He nodded. "Extenuating circumstances. You didn't answer any questions?"

"No."

"Good. Sit tight. Let me see what I can do."

"Also, I wasn't watching her the whole time I was in that neighborhood. I have a new boyfriend who lives nearby. Some of the time I was watching his house, waiting for him to get home. You can say I'm excessively punctual, if that helps me look less like a stalker."

He grinned. "Waiting in your car for your boyfriend to get home," he said with a nod. "How close is his house?"

"On the same block."

"Good. Will he confirm that you're in a relationship?"

"Yes, I assume so," she said. "Though he might think twice about it now that I'm a jailbird."

He smiled and gave her shoulder a squeeze. "By the way, did that swollen lip happen while you were in custody?"

"Yes," she said, showing him the shallow cut on the inside of her lip and the blood on her shirt. Then she told him what happened. "Will it help?"

"It will," he said.

BRINK STOOD on the back deck, staring at his phone. Callie hadn't answered his texts, which concerned him. Normally she answered immediately. Where would she be for three hours without the time to answer a text?

He kept thinking about the fact that she'd been investigating people. What if she'd found the perpetrator from the dream and confronted him? What if instead of Ashleigh, the guy had taken Callie?

There was a knot in Brink's stomach that would not go away. That first day he'd found out what she was doing, he'd told her to leave him out of it. He should've told her later that he'd changed his mind. He did not want her doing dangerous things alone.

Now he had no idea where she'd been all day. If she was in trouble, he didn't even know where to start looking.

He guessed he should begin with Ashleigh. Callie had been trying to get a look at the people around the girl. Ash, he thought with a frown. Their situation was really screwed up at the moment, and he didn't want to see her, but he couldn't let that stop him. He looked at his watch. He hoped Heather wasn't sauced up. She was hard to deal with when drunk.

His phone whistled, and he grabbed it. The text wasn't from Callie. It was from Heather.

Need to talk to you about your girlfriend.

Brink called her immediately.

"What's up?" he asked when she answered.

"Your girlfriend was at Ash's school today. She's been watching Ash at the gym and watching the house. Ashleigh didn't tell me all this until just now. So who the hell is your girlfriend, and what the hell's wrong with her?"

"Whatever happened, Ashleigh misinterpreted it."

"Well, we're about to get it sorted out. The school made a complaint, and she's been arrested."

Brink froze.

"The Kinley police have her in custody?"

"No, Granger Falls. Listen, I have to go. I just wanted you to know what's going on so you could decide if she's really someone you want to be involved with." She ended the call.

Brink went inside the house, locked the back door, and grabbed his keys.

At least her life wasn't in danger.

He drove to the Granger Falls police station and arrived at the same time Heather and Ashleigh did.

"What are you doing here?" Ashleigh asked, not hostile just surprised.

"Did you tell her?" he asked Heather.

Heather moved so that she was between them. "Go home, Brink. You don't belong here."

So no, she hadn't told Ash the truth yet. He took the

steps two at a time to reach the door first and then held it open for them.

"Thanks," Ashleigh said.

Heather glared at him.

In the station, he said, "Ashleigh, there are some things you and I need to talk about."

"Ok."

"Listen, you're not going to manipulate her into lying to the police. She's going to tell them the truth and whatever happens will happen."

"Fine," Brink said, though it wasn't fine with him. At all. He just didn't know if part of the reason that Ashleigh was pursuing this was because she was jealous that he had a girlfriend. Defending Callie in front of her might be like throwing gas on the fire. He needed to find out exactly what the police had charged her with.

Heather guided Ashleigh to the desk of an officer, but Brink didn't follow. He paused when a woman who stood next to another desk caught his eye. She was tiny, petite and thin, dressed in Levi's and a black T-shirt. Her hair was as dark as an oil slick, but her skin was as smooth and pale as alabaster. There was a flower tattoo on her inner forearm, and she had blue eyes that swallowed every detail of the scene. He had a feeling he knew who she was.

After a beat, she strode over. "Hey, I'm Callie's cousin Lotus. Are you him?"

"Greg Brinkman," he said, extending a hand. "Brink."

She shook his hand. "She said you were big. She's always exaggerating."

"She said you were dangerous. What do you when you get mad? Kick people with your size-five boots?"

Lotus had a smile like Callie's, with a little dimple in the corner. "She should be out in a minute."

"You sure? The accuser just showed up to give a statement."

Lotus glanced over. "That's the dream girl, huh?"

"The girl from Callie's dream, yeah. What did they arrest Callie for?"

Lotus grinned. "Stalking."

"What?"

"Don't worry. They're already re-thinking it."

"Why?"

"You don't think I came alone, do you? Here she comes," Lotus said.

Brink turned.

"What happened to your face?" Lotus and Brink asked in unison.

"You met?" Callie asked.

"We met. Who did that to your face?" Lotus asked.

"It was a misunderstanding."

"Agreed," Lotus said evenly. "In the cell? Or with one of these guys?"

"The cell."

"A girl. That makes it mine," she told Brink.

"No need. I took care of it myself," Callie said. "But thank you for coming." She hugged her cousin and then turned to the lawyer. "Are we good?"

He nodded. "Free to go."

Lotus touched the corner of Callie's mouth. "Needs a little time on ice. Who's driving you? Me or the mountain?"

"I am," Brink said.

"Okay," Lotus said. To Callie, she added, "Ice. Don't forget." She turned to him. "Nice meeting you, Brink. See you this weekend unless she gets arrested again before then."

"She's kidding. I never get arrested twice in one week."

Lotus winked and walked away.

Callie shook hands with the lawyer and thanked him. He told her it was his pleasure and that he'd be in touch if there were more questions. After which, Brink hustled her out of the station.

"Are you all right?" he asked when they were on the road back to her place.

"Yeah, I'm fine. It was my first time getting arrested. Not gonna lie. I was scared when they booked me and locked me in that cell." She exhaled with a shake of her head. "At least they didn't formally charge me. I don't think they will."

"Tell me what happened."

"I didn't want you involved. How did you end up at the station?"

"First, tell me what happened."

She nodded and spilled the beans. It turned out there wasn't much more to the story than what he already knew.

"So you basically walked around, while supervised by an administrator, and then you left?"

"Yes."

He shook his head. "The police chief really does not like you."

She shrugged.

He filled her in on getting the text from Heather and their subsequent conversation.

"I don't blame Ashleigh for reporting me," Callie said. "She doesn't know what's going on. But Heather's a different story. She's furious at me for parking on the street and watching the houses? She didn't ask you why? Even after last night when she cried on my shoulder, literally?"

"Didn't ask a thing."

Callie shook her head. "I'm tired of these people. I'm going home. I'm having honey-glazed ham for dinner and then cake and a glass of wine. Or two. And unless Ashleigh is actually abducted tonight, I'm not going to think about her for the next twenty-four hours. I'm done."

"Good," Brink said.

23

Callie and Brink had two great days and nights. He stayed at her place. They cooked together, played with the dog, and talked and made love till late at night. He slept in, worked out, and worked, distracted toward the end of the day because he wanted to get back to her.

This was the life he wanted, one where they were together every night.

He confided that he'd begun to believe she really did have some form of extrasensory perception. He told her that during the second night, while asleep, she'd said very clearly, "I don't know why you threw away those Captain America underwear she got you. You could've kept them as a souvenir."

He'd forgotten about the skivvies Jen had bought him, mocking him for his plan to enlist. They'd been Captain America briefs with the shield over the crotch. He never wore cartoon underwear or briefs, and he'd been offended by her condescension. He'd tossed the briefs in a commercial garbage can on the way home. They'd never talked about them again, so it was hard to believe that nineteen years later Callie could've found out about them the way anyone without psychic powers would have. He hadn't seen Jen in years. He'd heard she'd moved to Seattle.

Of course, it wasn't definitive proof of Callie's abilities. He was holding onto some skepticism, but it was fading fast.

At the moment, he'd woken from a dead sleep, and something felt off. The room was cold. He turned on the bedside lamp and found Callie sitting up in bed, staring at nothing, her breathing shallow.

"Callie?"

She didn't answer. Rufus ran up to the door and began to bark.

"Callie. Callista!" he said, shaking her. The vacant look and twitching around her mouth scared him. Was she having some sort of seizure?

He fumbled for his phone on the nightstand when she spoke.

"He has her."

By the time Brink turned, she was out of bed. She jerked the door open. "Here we go, Rufus. Stay calm. It'll be all right." She rubbed the dog's head.

Brink jerked the covers back and got up. Why the hell was it so cold in the room?

He followed her lead and dressed.

"No, Brink. You stay here. Just Rufus and I will go. I'll call you when I know something."

"Like hell," Brink said, grabbing his gun.

She pulled a sweatshirt on, stopping to hold the wall. "I know something. In the dream, I saw his truck in the parking lot of the school. There's a book on the passenger seat. It's...something." She closed her eyes.

Rufus barked and turned circles in the doorway, ready to run.

"Hang on," Brink told the dog.

"American Government. He teaches History or Social Science. She knows him."

She opened her eyes. "I'm not sure where he's taking her, but I saw the Kinley bowling alley and the Starbucks."

"North side of town, right where the feeder is. He's about to get on the interstate," Brink said.

"Yes. He can't stay around here. Too many people know them." Callie shuddered, then turned toward the dog. "Come on, Rufus, let's go find her." Callie rushed down the stairs. Brink and the dog followed. She grabbed her shoes and yanked them on.

"Brink, you don't have to come."

"Don't say that again."

She paused in the middle of tying her shoes to look up at him.

"Your life is my life. Where you go, I go. Period."

"All right," she said. "But you have to let us work, me and Rufus. We know how to do this. You can't distract us."

"I won't do anything to jeopardize the mission."

"The mission," she said with a nod. "The mission is to get Ashleigh back before he does something to her. It's not to protect me and Rufus. You understand that, right? She's the highest priority."

"I understand," he said, but acknowledgment wasn't agreement. Ashleigh could be Callie's highest priority, but she couldn't be his.

She sucked in a breath. "She's scared. In the dream, she was really scared. She called for you."

That was a kick in the gut. Brink yanked the laces on his boots and tied them. He wished he'd been close enough to hear Ashleigh call him. He wished he'd had the chance to drop the guy who'd grabbed her. He strode to the door and pulled it open. The police chief stood on the walkway.

"You're up late," the man said.

"No time," Callie said, rushing past him and down the stairs. "Rufus, let's go." The dog bolted past the chief.

"I need to talk to you."

"Brink, if you're coming, let's go," she said, ignoring the cop.

"I said to stop. If you don't answer my questions, I'll arrest you."

Brink hit the key fob to unlock the truck. Callie pulled the passenger door open. The chief pulled out his gun and started to raise it.

Brink had him in a chokehold before he had time to consider the consequences. He tightened his grip until the chief lost consciousness and slumped to the ground. Then Brink jogged over to the truck, got in, and fired it up.

"He's not—?"

"Just unconscious."

"They must know she's missing. He came to see if we had her."

"Think so?" Brink asked, backing out and then gunning it.

"Yes. He wouldn't have pulled his gun to talk about my trespassing on school property three days ago."

"You're right about that."

"It's good. The more people looking for her the better," Callie said. "But I'm sorry that you insisted on being involved. An altercation with the police chief is not good. Sorry."

"Couldn't be helped."

"Even so, we're going to say that Rufus knocked him down, not you."

"All right," Brink said, knowing that it wouldn't fly. They'd cross that bridge when they came to it.

24

Brink drove for forty minutes, breaking the speed limit the entire time. If there was an APB for his truck, they weren't doing themselves any favors by barreling down the highway.

"We have to speed to catch up. I don't think he's speeding. He won't want to be noticed. I need to catch him before he gets to the woods," Callie said.

"What woods?"

"I don't know. I just know if he gets her into the woods, I won't find her in time."

"Meaning what?" The guy would rape Ashleigh? Kill her? Both?

Brink felt like puking. He kept thinking that maybe if he'd paid more attention to her, she might not have gone looking for attention from some middle-aged school teacher who'd become obsessed with her. Brink knew the situation wasn't his fault, but he still felt responsible. He'd been busy covering his own ass, and now a teenage girl was in the hands of a very bad man.

His heart pounded like he was going into battle, but so

far there was no one to fight, no buildings to clear, no hostages to rescue.

He also had no idea where they were going. He was driving blind, all his faith in the woman in the passenger seat whose eyes were closed.

THIS WAS TOTALLY NEW. Callie felt a connection to the missing girl, which had never happened before. Was that because she'd actually met Ashleigh?

"She's crying. He's gagged her. She's under covers and boxes. She can't see anything and no one can see her. They're stopped."

"Where, Cal? A gas station? A rest stop? What do you see?" Brink demanded.

"We can't see anything. We're under so much stuff. It's hard to breathe. This rag tastes metallic...smells like turpentine. I can't breathe. I smell something else. Not chemicals," she murmured and then paused. "It's food. Fried food." Callie's eyes popped open. "We're close. Slow down."

"Slow down as in get off the expressway?"

"No, just get in the right lane. Drive the speed limit."

Rufus's big head came forward and his drool-dampened chin rested on the dash. Callie placed a hand on the back of the dog's neck.

"It'll be tricky, Ruf. It's not just finding one this time."

Brink bristled silently. He was the armed Marine. Why did she seem to be putting more faith in the dog's ability to help than his?

They approached a sign for an exit with food, gas, and lodging. She stiffened, and the dog growled in response.

"Chicken. That's what I smelled. Take that exit."

He saw a Church's Chicken that advertised a late-night drive thru and moved into the right lane.

"Those lights. I saw them in the dream," she said, pointing to a gas station on the other side of the median dividing the highway. "Okay," she said, grabbing her purse from the floor and digging through it. "Park along the fence, not too far back. I don't want him to get suspicious."

He swung the truck around, drove into the lot and pulled into a spot. Callie unbuckled her seatbelt and turned to look over at him.

"There was a fountain drink. If he's inside, we might be able to get her to safety without confronting him."

Callie was holding something in her hand. Brink leaned forward to look and realized it was a Taser. For God's sake. She'd have to be right on top of the guy to use that. No way was he letting her get that close to the asshole.

"You should be the one to look inside. He could've seen me at the school or in the parking lot the day I was there," she said. "He might recognize me."

"Sure," he said, not bothering to say that it wasn't logical for him to check the gas station since he couldn't confirm identification even if the enemy was inside. He bet if she wanted him to go into the gas station on his own, it was so she could approach the guy's car alone.

If the guy had gotten fast food and was eating it before he gassed up and got back on the interstate, he'd park as far back as possible. He wouldn't want other cars too close in case Ashleigh made noise. Brink knew Callie had thought the same thing because she kept looking toward the north-east corner, which away from the big lights of the pumps.

"Stay in the car," he said.

She nodded.

He strode to the mini-mart and went inside. He scanned the aisles, then slipped back out and went the far way around the building. He spotted the truck with the cab. The interior light was on and a man sat in the driver's seat.

Brink heard a hiss of air and squinted. Callie had punctured a tire. Smart. Now if the guy tried to drive off, he wouldn't get far.

But Jesus Christ. She was going for the driver's side door.

Brink sprinted toward them as she tapped on the glass.

The guy rolled down the window, but didn't make eye contact.

"Can you spare some change? I lost my wallet. I just need enough gas to get home."

"No," he said, looking straight ahead and leaning away from the window. He didn't want her to see his face.

"Come on, you must have fifty cents or a dollar you can spare. Please," she begged. She sounded so convincing.

"I said no!" he snapped.

"All right. You don't have to yell," she said, walking away.

What was she doing? Was he the guy? It had better be, or she owed him a new tire. Brink stayed in the shadows, but in less than a minute Callie returned to the door on the driver's side.

She tapped the window again. This time the guy shoved the door open, knocking her back.

Brink raised his gun.

"I told you to get the hell out of here!"

From her place on the ground Callie said, "I just wanted to tell you that you have a flat tire!"

"What?" he snapped.

She regained her feet and bent over to brush the dirt off herself. The guy got out of the truck. As he passed, her arm shot out and she made contact. The Taser hummed, and the guy crumpled to the ground.

As cool as if she'd been born to do it, she reached in and grabbed the guy's keys. She strode to the back and unlocked the truck. She raised the cab's rear window and lowered the tailgate. Rufus stood at attention, completely silent. It was unbelievable that the dog had stayed so still and quiet when the man had shouted.

Callie climbed in the back. The guy on the ground stirred. Rufus growled and came to the edge of the truck.

Brink emerged from the shadows, his gun trained on the man.

"Stay down," Brink said in a low voice.

"Hey, what's going on? Hey! Hey!" a voice coming from an approaching car yelled.

Brink jerked his head to see a guy with black-rimmed glasses. To the motorist, it might look like a robbery.

"Don't shoot! We've called the police," the man said.

Brink was only distracted for a second, but it gave the asshole time to roll under the truck.

Brink dropped to a knee and tipped sideways to get eyes on the guy. He saw the gun just before the flash.

He fell and rolled to get cover behind the front wheel. He heard footsteps. The asshole was up. He didn't want him rounding the truck to get to Callie. Brink regained his feet and circled to the back, but the guy wasn't coming for Callie. He was running toward a fence.

From inside the truck, a girl screamed. He looked in and saw Ashleigh, disheveled and terrified, wrists and ankles bound.

"It's okay. You're okay now," Callie said.

Ashleigh saw him and lurched toward him as best she

could. He reached in and grabbed her. Ash put her arms over his neck and fell against him, sobbing.

Rufus's barking drew their attention. The dog ran toward the fence.

"Rufus, no!" Callie said, jumping off the tailgate and racing after him.

He jerked Ashleigh's arms off his neck. "I'll be right back, baby. Let me get this guy."

The side of her white shirt was smudged with blood. *That fucking bastard.*

"Don't leave! Please don't leave!"

Bystanders were there, watching and no doubt filming. "Call nine one one," Brink shouted. "I'll be right back, Ash. You're all right," he said as he took off toward the fence. He heard the crack of a gunshot and sprinted toward the sound.

He spotted the guy. Thirty yards away. His gun arm snapped up.

Center mass. Brink squeezed the trigger. *Pop. Pop.*

The guy went down and stayed down. *Good.*

When Brink found Callie, she had Rufus cradled in her arms. "What did I tell you? Just the girl. No going after the guy unless he attacked us. We got her. You didn't have to chase him," she said to the dog, tears streaming down her face. "You had to be a hero. Well, this time I'm not going to let them give you a medal."

The dog panted. Brink knelt down next to them.

"Oh no!" she screamed, letting go of Rufus. "No, no." She jumped forward and grabbed Brink. It wasn't until he saw the blood that he realized he'd been hit.

Her fear and grief were spiraling.

"I'm all right. Callie!" he barked. "I'm all right."

She blinked, silent for a moment. "Swear?"

"Yeah, I've been wounded badly. I know how that feels. This ain't it."

"Can you walk back to the witnesses in the parking lot? I need help carrying Rufus. He's hurt pretty bad."

She took a deep breath and swallowed down her tears. *Good girl.*

Brink put the gun away, stood, and bent over to pick up the dog.

"Don't you do it. Exerting yourself will make you bleed more. Don't you know anything?"

He smiled but ignored her. He carried the dog back to the parking lot and laid him down on the blacktop. Rufus had been hit in the shoulder, but the bullet might have gone into his chest.

The police and ambulances arrived.

When the paramedics confirmed that Brink's blood pressure was normal, he took off his bloody shirt to reveal a flesh wound.

Callie was satisfied that he wasn't dying because she eased back. "You go with them. I have to get Rufus to an emergency vet," she said.

"I know one," the medic said. "Come on. We can drop the dog on the way."

"That's against the rules," the driver said.

"Special circumstances. Brink, put him in the back. Where's Ashleigh?" Callie asked, then realized they were loading her into another ambulance. "You should ride with her, Brink."

Brink settled the huge mutt on the stretcher and glanced over at Ashleigh, shell-shocked and pale, as photographs were taken.

"You think I should?"

"Yes, definitely."

He kissed the top of Callie's head and then walked to the other ambulance. He climbed in with Ash.

He held out a hand to ward off the questions they were firing from all sides. "I'm the dad," he said. *At least for tonight,* he thought.

EPILOGUE

C allie had lied. She did let the dog get a medal.

Rufus had had emergency surgery and recovered just fine on a diet of steak and honey-glazed pork chops. He accepted his new medal with good grace, but whenever it was within reach he chewed on it rather than wearing it.

Upon finding out that Brink was not her dad, Ashleigh became distant and quiet for a time. When Brink texted her to workout with him, though, she returned to the gym. Soon, she was his morning lifting partner.

Heather still drank and was terrified of Rufus, but she had also started therapy and even conceded that not all dogs were bad all the time.

Police Chief Pell never made a report about his trip to Callie Melville's house on the night they rescued Ashleigh from her abductor. Ashleigh and the school withdrew their complaints against Callie and sent a joint letter of thanks for her part in recognizing a predator in their midst and stopping him from escaping with Ashleigh to the cabin in the woods that he'd stocked for a prolonged stay.

The first story about the abduction and rescue made the front page, but when the follow-up piece was relegated to page three, Mrs. Phyllis Brinkman wrote a strongly worded letter to the *Kinley-Granger Falls Sentinel* over its placement. She said heroes were always front page news. Though the paper's response was kind, she was unsatisfied.

She said she didn't have time to fool around with the paper, though. She'd decided that her grandson and his lady love should have a ceremony honoring them at Kinley Town Hall. So Phyllis was making plans to pursue the matter by consulting her new friend, Country Club Ken, his attorney, and the governor.

THANK you for reading *Kissing the Suspect*, the first story in the Mystical Melville series! If you enjoyed it, I think you'll also enjoy the humorous fantasies in my Southern Witch series.

I'd love to connect with you in any way you like to be reached. To find out about new releases, sign up for my newsletter at https://www.frostfiction.com/newsletter

OTHER WAYS FOR US TO CONNECT...

Like my FB author page: https://www.facebook.com/AuthorKimberlyFrost

Or visit my website at FrostFiction.com for links to follow or friend me on Instagram, Twitter, Goodreads & BookBub. You can also email through my website. I love to hear from readers!

I appreciate your help in spreading the word, including

telling a friend. Reviews help readers find books! Please leave a review on your favorite book site.

ABOUT THE AUTHOR

Kimberly Frost is the national bestselling author of the humorous Southern Witch series. In 2010, she won the PEARL award for best new paranormal author. Her books vary in tone, but always blend romance and mystery. They have been Barnes & Noble Recommended Reads and Romantic Times Top Picks. This is Kimberly's eighth novel.

facebook.com/AuthorKimberlyFrost

twitter.com/FrostFiction

instagram.com/author_kfrost

ALSO BY KIMBERLY FROST

Made in the USA
Lexington, KY
31 January 2019